BECAUSE YOU SAID YES

A WILLOW BAY NOVEL

KELLY COLLINS

BOOK NOOK PRESS

Copyright © 2023 by Kelley Maestas

No part of this publication may be reproduced, distributed, or transmitted in any form or by any means, including photocopying, recording, or other electronic or mechanical methods, without the prior written permission of the publisher, except as permitted by U.S. copyright law. For permission requests, contact kelly@authorkellycollins.com.
The story, all names, characters, and incidents portrayed in this production are fictitious. No identification with actual persons (living or deceased), places, buildings, and products is intended or should be inferred. All products or brand names are trademarks of their respective owners.

CHAPTER ONE

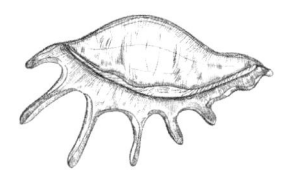

Charlotte Sutton stood in front of her new storefront window and smiled. Because You Said Yes was no longer a dream but a reality. Whoever said you couldn't make pretty with a bit of lipstick hadn't met her or her bag of tricks. She took an old, abandoned storefront on Main Street and, with a little elbow grease, paint, and decals, turned it into a dream bridal planning boutique.

It was the first time she'd created something of her own. The first time she wasn't handed an opportunity. The first time she took a chance on herself. It was also the first time she'd put everything at risk—her home, her savings, her reputation. She was a damn fool, or maybe a genius. Only time would tell.

She walked inside and breathed in the scent of lavender. It was supposed to be a calming scent, but her hummingbird heart hadn't gotten the message. She walked past the wall of linens and the table of handmade papers to place her bag under the counter. She turned on the crystal lamps and picked a stray blonde hair from the plush chair where she hoped her second client would sit and plan their perfect day.

She questioned why she thought she could start a bridal shop. Perhaps it was due to Emmaline's wedding turning out beautifully. She knew she was getting older and could not make a living peddling beauty products and makeovers forever. The last job she had was doing Mabel Pickleby's makeup for her funeral. While Mabel didn't look a day over ninety, despite being a hundred and five when she passed, Charlotte didn't want her future to be less alive than her clients.

A knock at the door startled her, making her jump a few inches off the glazed concrete floor.

"Come and open the door." Her best friend, Emmaline, held a tray of coffees and a Cricket's Diner box in her hands. It was hard not to think of her as a Brown, but since her wedding to Miles she was now a McClintock. "I come bearing gifts."

Charlotte knew she could count on her friends to join her on opening day. She wouldn't be allowed to open her doors and chew her fingernails to the nubs, worrying about how she would pay her next loan payment.

Her heels tip-tapped across the floor in a sharp staccato sound as she made her way back to the door, turned the closed sign to open, and swung the door wide enough for Emmaline and her box to clear the entry.

"Welcome to Because You Said Yes," Charlotte said in her sweetest voice. "Let me help you before you drop those drinks and put me in debtor's prison with everything the coffee will destroy." This wasn't a discount wedding shop. While she'd do her darnedest to get the best deal for her client, high-end was where her tastes sat and where she wanted to dabble. Nothing in her shop was standard. If a person could afford a planner, they could afford the pretties. Why be average when you could be extra?

Her mama used to tell her she could marry a rich man as easily as a poor man. Hell, her mama had married wealthy twice. One union lasted about six seconds, but the second a lifetime. Charlotte had never found any man worth marrying. They simply didn't offer enough in exchange for a life sentence. But she loved a good wedding and opening Because You Said Yes would allow her to repeatedly experience the wedding of her dreams or someone else's.

"What did you bring?"

"Cricket made you Mexican wedding cookies and a fresh pot of chicory coffee." She leaned in and whispered, "It's that private stock she keeps in the back for her special friends."

Charlotte took the tray of coffees and set them on the counter. "It better not be that cat poop coffee she's always trying to get us to drink."

"It's not. That's called Kopi Luwak."

"It's cat shit coffee, no matter how you brew it." She took the lid off the cup and breathed in the steam. Not that she didn't trust Emmaline, but she wouldn't put it past Cricket to trick her into trying something new. "Why do we have four cups?" After smelling the chicory, she deemed it safe to sip. The bitter grounds mixed nicely with her anxiety as the warm liquid eased down her throat to hit like a ball of acid in her gut.

"Because we're expecting company. This is a big deal and requires a celebration and all celebrations include your friends."

Just then, the door opened, and in walked Marybeth,

looking like she was going to a funeral in her mostly black Chanel suit.

"Did someone die?" Charlotte said a silent prayer that no one in town had passed today. She made sure to pick a good day to open her business. It wasn't a Friday, the 13th, or one of the historically unlucky days of the year. It was a simple Wednesday in September. Though she'd missed the summer bride frenzy, she hoped that people would continue to marry throughout the year as they always did and choose her shop for planning their perfect day. Since weddings took months to organize, she was in the perfect position to snag all of next summer's brides.

"Not yet, but after we celebrate your beginning, I'll visit your neighbor. She's taken a turn for the worse and nearing the end."

Charlotte only had two neighbors. One was Dr. Robinson, and the other was a woman she hadn't had time to get to know. "Who's taken a turn for the worse?"

"Chloe Richmond." Marybeth stared at her like she'd lost her mind. "You know, the woman with breast cancer who has a sweet little girl named Ivy? She's not going to make it."

Charlotte nearly dropped her coffee, but Emmaline took it from her hands as it tipped. "My neighbor is dying, and I didn't know it?"

"In your defense," Marybeth started. "You had a lot going on this summer with Brie and Emmaline. When you put your mind to Because You Said Yes, you've thought of nothing since. You're like a dog with a bone."

"And it's about time," Emmaline added. "No one deserves a happy ending as much as you do. You've always put others first."

"Right, but I've got a dying neighbor, and I didn't know

it." There were many things Charlotte was, but inconsiderate was not one of them. She was the model for Southern hospitality. Why hadn't she spent more time getting to know her neighbor? She couldn't even place her face. There was some recollection of a young girl running along the beach, but that could have been anyone's child. "Give me one of those cookies so I can sweeten the sour feeling in my stomach." What was going on with her? In her attempt to find a slice of happiness for herself, she'd turned into someone she didn't know. She'd done things she promised she'd never do, like hawk her house to the hilt, bury herself in debt, and take risks with her future. She wasn't a risk taker, and there were things an intelligent woman should never do. Maybe starting over at fifty should be one of them. "I'm an awful person."

"No, you're a woman finding her way to her true self." Emmaline walked to the wall where a beautiful wedding dress was draped perfectly over a mannequin. "Are you sure you didn't win the lottery? This dress alone had to cost ten grand."

"Twelve," Charlotte said with pride. It was the only dress she had in the store, but it was the dress of her dreams. She promised herself on day one that her business would reflect her dreams and the weddings she planned would be for her clients'. As she looked around the shop, it was everything she'd find on her dream day, from giant white magnolia blossoms to the custom beaded gown hanging on display.

"How did you afford this?" Emmaline let her fingers run over the beaded bodice before she turned to face Charlotte.

"My first gig was a smash." She'd never tell her friend that she gave her everything at cost. Emmaline's wedding wasn't about making money, but about gaining courage. "Did you ever find your shoe?" She shuddered to think what that dog had done with her friend's left shoe. She'd never heard of a dog with a shoe fetish, and certainly not one who could differentiate between left and right, and only stole the left ones.

Emmaline shook her head. "No, I'm fairly certain Ollie buried it, but it'll turn up again. He always brings things back for another run. Just the other day, I found my left beaded sandal. I lost that at the Brown Resort before it burned down. The dog is magical that way."

"Speaking of the resort, how is it going at The Kessler for Brie and Carter?"

Charlotte expected to see sadness in Emmaline's eyes. She'd lived for her family's resort, and when it burned down, so did all her dreams. Or maybe what burned were others' expectations. Looking into her friend's eyes, all she saw was satisfaction and pride. There wasn't an ounce of regret.

"It's great. Carter and Brie melded the properties together to make it uniquely theirs, and I'm so proud of them. The new park is beautiful and taking down the old boathouse and dock opened up the space for the guests to enjoy the beach. It's more than anyone could have expected."

Expectations were a tricky thing. She was born and raised with none except to smile and look pretty. She always thought she was the lucky one, but maybe if someone had expected more from her, she would have been motivated to go after it. The truth was, she should have expected more from herself. Winning Miss Lone Star State by default shouldn't be anyone's only claim to fame.

"Should we close up shop and visit my neighbor?"

Marybeth frowned. "You are not closing your door twenty minutes after you opened it. What does that say about you?"

"It says that I care more about people than things." She picked up her coffee and took a drink. Rather than focus on the soothing warmth, she latched on to the bitter chicory as it washed over her taste buds. "You're not even her neighbor, and you're visiting."

Marybeth tugged on the hem of her jacket. "I'm going over as a liaison for the church. I have paperwork to drop off."

"So sad to be so young and lose a battle with the big C." Emmaline hung her head. "And to think I told Brie I had it when it was crow's feet I was suffering from. It makes me feel like an awful person." She took a cookie from the box and shoved the whole thing in her mouth. Powdered sugar poofed into the air when she breathed out, making Marybeth step back. She brushed away the dusting of it that settled on her black jacket.

"And that little girl she's leaving behind. Her name is Ivy, and she's as cute as a ladybug," Marybeth said.

"Where's the father?" Charlotte asked.

Both Marybeth and Emmaline lifted their shoulders.

"She isn't from here, so we don't have the 4-1-1 on her, but she's got a nanny, and I'm sure someone will come to the rescue. Let's hope they get here soon."

The door opened, and in walked Cricket and Tilly. Cricket brought her own cup of coffee. Not the paper cup she filled for them but a diner mug that read, *Sometimes you need to say Cluck It, and walk away.*

"Look at this place," Cricket said. "It's fancier than an updo at your first cotillion."

Charlotte tried to see the place through her friends'

eyes, but all she saw when she looked at the linens, the sample invitations, and the fresh floral arrangements was the minimum payment she'd be hard-pressed to make on next month's credit card bill. She had a bougie appetite on a bologna budget.

"If I ever get married," Tilly said. "You're planning my wedding."

Charlotte laughed. "Well, I'd hope so, being I'm one of your best friends." She smiled and buried all self-doubt. There was no room for it in her life. This had to work, or she was screwed.

Tilly looked at her watch and dug a bottle of champagne from her bag. "It might be nine o'clock in Willow Bay, but it's five o'clock somewhere. Shall we toast to new beginnings and dreams coming true?"

CHAPTER TWO

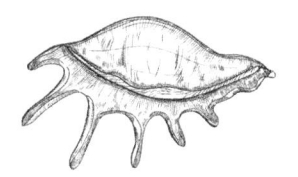

Bastien Richmond stared out the window of the small beach cottage his sister had bought that summer. It was easier looking at the waves lapping at the shore than at Chloe, who had wasted away to nothing.

"Look at me," her weak voice pleaded.

He slowly turned to face her. Gone were the long locks of chestnut hair that used to frame her face. A smiling emoji bandana covered her bald head. Her eyes had slipped farther back into their sockets, as if they were saying farewell first. He'd been visiting as often as he could, but the weeks that passed since his last visit hadn't been kind to his sister. She told him she was dying, and he chose to believe she'd live, but looking at her now, he realized she'd never lied to him.

"What can I do?" His voice quivered, so he cleared his throat to cover his emotions.

"I told you what I needed."

He closed his eyes. "Please don't ask me to do that."

She patted the bed beside her. "You're her only chance."

He scrubbed his face with his palm and sat. "How can

you say that? What do I know about raising a child? According to our mother, I'm still one."

She laughed a little, but it made her cough, which racked her insides until she lay limp against her propped-up pillows. "You need to promise me you'll take her. No matter what, you'll fight for her. Mom is going to come after her. You know it, and I know it. Promise me you'll do whatever it takes to ensure she doesn't get to raise my girl."

It felt like the world had taken a vacuum and sucked his insides out. Chloe didn't know what she was asking. He wanted to reach over and loosen her bandana. It had to be cutting off the oxygen to her brain. "Chloe, think about it. Mom raised you and me, and we turned out okay."

She breathed deeply and seemed to sink into the mattress when she exhaled. "I want Ivy to know she has options. If she wants to be the president, I want her to think she has a chance. Mom would ask her the president of what? And then lead her to the bridge club."

He couldn't argue with his sister. They'd been raised by a woman who could have penned every book on marrying well, and then wrote the sequel called *Married and Miserable.* Annette Richmond wanted what she wanted and got exactly what she asked for. She was wealthy and lived in a beautiful house in Atlanta. She had hundreds of friends and was the loneliest person he knew. He understood why his sister didn't want Ivy raised by their mother, but he wasn't the best alternative.

"There's got to be a better choice for her."

His sister gripped his hand and sat up. He stared at the determination in her eyes—eyes which had once been the color of the Caribbean sea but had washed out to something gray and lifeless. But in that second, they were fierce and stormy.

"There is no other choice. Promise me, Bastien. If you do nothing else for me, promise me you'll raise Ivy. You are a good man."

A tear slipped down his cheek, but he swiped it away as fast as it fell. "I am exactly like our father. I'm married to my work."

She gripped both of his hands. "You are not our father, but I don't want her to grow up and be our mother—bitter, angry, and unsatisfied. Promise me." She held so tightly onto his hands that he couldn't let go—couldn't separate himself from his sister's dying wish.

A head of chestnut hair blowing in the breeze caught his attention as he watched Ivy run ahead of her nanny toward the water. She was happy despite the circumstances. She was Chloe thirty-five years ago. Back when their lives were somewhat normal. Back before his father took on a string of lovers, and his mother turned to vodka martinis and pool boys for pleasure. Back when family meant something.

Chloe squeezed his hands again, and he took his eyes off Ivy to look at her. He would do anything for her, and she knew it. So, he smiled and swallowed the lump of uncertainty lodged in his throat. "I promise."

She relaxed and let out a sigh. "Thank you. Now I can go in peace." She stared out the window and watched Ivy collect seashells from the shore. Several minutes later, Ivy ran toward the house with Rachel, her nanny, racing to catch up.

How was he supposed to do what he did and raise a five-year-old? He spent most of his life on an airplane going from deal to deal. Chloe had no idea what she was asking, and then maybe she did. She'd been on him to slow down and take a breath, but he hated the silence and loneliness that came with a break, so he stayed on the fast train all the time, racing toward the next deal.

"Isn't it time to enjoy the scenic route?" Chloe asked, as if reading his mind.

Ivy raced in and hopped onto the hospital bed. She crawled over her mother and threw herself into Bastien's arms. "Uncle Bast, you're here."

He clung to her. "I'm here, little bug. I'm here, and I'm not going anywhere."

Ivy let go and fell back to the bed, snuggling up to her mother's side. "Mommy is leaving us soon, and she told me I have to take care of you."

His heart twisted. Maybe that was the plan all along. Leave it to Chloe to twist the plot and the narrative. "We'll take care of each other."

With Ivy in her arms and Bastien by her side, Chloe fell asleep while they stared at the ocean in the distance. Like the tides, life rolled in and out. Each time the water lapped on shore, it was a rebirth for the sand and all that lived below. Life had a cycle, like a sea with high and low tides. The day Chloe left the world would be the lowest tide of his life, but she'd leave behind Ivy, who would carry on the cycle. She'd be like the moon and rule the tides of his life from that point forward.

A soft knock came from the door. When he looked down at his sister and Ivy, they were both asleep, so he let go of Chloe's frail hand and answered the door.

Standing there was a woman dressed all in black, and it pissed him off. "Can I help you?" He stepped outside the door and closed it behind him. "What do you want?" His badass boardroom voice took over, and the woman stepped back.

"I'm Marybeth Davidson, the pastor's wife."

He hadn't known his sister to be religious and couldn't imagine what this woman was doing on the doorstep. "We're not interested in what you're selling. She isn't dead yet." His gut wrenched so hard he nearly doubled over from the pain.

"Oh, darlin', I'm not selling anything. I'm delivering paperwork and good tidings." She opened her purse and took out an envelope and a bag of white sugar-coated cookies. "And a treat for Ivy."

He felt awful for assuming the worst. "I'm sorry, but it's a trying time for my family."

She set her hand on his shoulder and left it there. "Chloe made all her arrangements. I'm assuming you're her brother?"

He nodded. "I'm Bastien." He stared down at the envelope. "Is that her will?"

She shook her head. "Oh no, we don't do legal work at the church. We do God's work. She wanted the funeral details. As for her will and stuff, I'm sure she's got that all together. She seems like the kind of woman to have a plan."

She was right. Chloe had her life all planned out, but then she always had. Their mother had picked out a husband for Chloe. Knowing Annette Richmond, she probably had the flowers and invitations ordered for the wedding when Chloe was still in her womb. But after college, Chloe had other plans. She wasn't interested in marrying well. She wanted to live life to the fullest and hopped on a plane to Paris. She traveled for a good fifteen years as a freelance journalist until she returned to the United States pregnant with Ivy. She says it was a sperm donor, but he was pretty sure that Chloe had all that planned out, too. She didn't pick a pretty boy out from a book, but probably chose from a long list of attributes she found attractive, like honesty and integrity. She never cared about what was in someone's bank account. It was what they held in their heart that mattered. The only thing she didn't plan was breast cancer that had metastasized.

"She's a force to be reckoned with." That part was true and why he thought she'd beat cancer.

"Anyway," Marybeth said. "Is she around, or should I leave this with you?"

He looked over his shoulder at the closed door. "She's sleeping. I'll make sure she gets it."

Marybeth nodded. "Is there anything I can do for you?"

He stared out at the water. "When you come back here again, can you not wear black? My sister is a vibrant soul, and I want whatever part of her life that's left to be filled with color."

Marybeth's eyes widened. "Oh my. I never considered."

"Well, I never considered a lot of things before today." He'd never considered having a family. Not one of his own, anyway. He'd seen what love did to people. It destroyed them. Nope, it was better to batten down the hatches and waterproof the heart because once you let people in, they had a way of drowning you. He'd seen love destroy enough people to know it wasn't for him. The only person he'd ever loved was Chloe until Ivy came along. How could one not love her? Now Chloe was leaving, and his heart ached. Was Ivy a lifeline, or was she an anchor that would eventually pull him under, too?

"You're not alone." She pointed to the big house on the right. "Dr. Robinson is right next door. I know she's been stopping by daily to check on your sister." She pointed to the home on the left side of his sister's property. "That house belongs to Charlotte. She's been busy lately, but don't hesitate to ask her for anything. She's one of the kindest women I know." Marybeth looked at his left hand. "And she's single too."

"I'm not looking." He couldn't wait to get out of the matchmaking South, where a best friend or a mama was always ready to take him off the market.

"It's when you're not looking that you're likely to be finding." She handed him the envelope and the cookies. "Squeeze Ivy for me and don't be a stranger. I'm right around the corner. You can't miss the building. It's the white one with a cross on the steeple." She turned to walk away but stopped. "Don't forget about Charlotte. That girl can turn a pig into a princess. If you need something, she'll find it. She's a good egg."

He waved and walked inside to find Rachel calling 911.

Ivy walked over and took his hand. In her little trembling voice, she said, "It's just you and me, kid." She buried her head against his hip and cried.

CHAPTER THREE

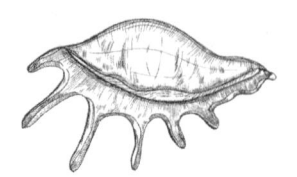

As far as first days went, Charlotte couldn't complain. Sometimes it wasn't about counting the wins but tallying up the losses that didn't occur. There wasn't a flood or a hurricane. Of those who walked inside the shop, no one tripped and fell and would sue her tomorrow for negligence. She didn't land a big wedding, but she talked to Sara Brighton about her daughter's future nuptials. Poor Danika wasn't even in high school, and her mother was already planning. She supposed that should make her happy because Southern mamas and weddings would be her lifeblood, but something sat heavy on her heart today, and she couldn't pinpoint what that was.

Marybeth walked inside and sank into a chair before she burst into tears.

"What in the world?" Charlotte rushed over and took the seat beside her friend. "Are you okay?"

Marybeth swiped at the tears and nodded. "Your neighbor passed. I went there like I said I would. I met the brother and gave him Chloe's plan. She had picked out the readings and the music and she wanted to have it in her end-of-life folder."

"Wait. She died?" Charlotte sucked in her breath.

"Have you not listened to me?"

"I heard you. I'm just clarifying." Maybe that was the heaviness that sat in the air around her all day. Her mama always told her she was a feeling person because she always knew when her friends were unhappy or when someone was sad. The emotions sat in the air like a fog that only she could see. "That's so sad. How old was she?"

Marybeth flopped back against the chair. "She was forty, with a five-year-old. Can you imagine?"

"I can't." What a nightmare. When Charlotte was younger, she had plenty of dreams. She'd get married by twenty-five and have two children by thirty. The first would be a boy to make his father proud and the second would be a girl, so her life would be complete. None of her dreams came true, but then she imagined that poor woman's didn't either. "Do they need food?" She thought about what was in her freezer. Any good Southern girl worth her salt had a dish waiting for an event, whether it be a death, a birth, or an intervention. Nothing said I care like a casserole.

"I'm starting a meal train. Shall I sign you up?"

"I'll take tonight." It was better to get it done and out of the way. Until she helped with something, she'd feel like she was useless. "I'll make my famous chicken and dumplings."

Marybeth stared at her. "It's only famous because you sent three people to the emergency room with food poisoning the last time you made it."

"I didn't defrost the chicken on the counter this go around. It's been in the refrigerator the entire time." She got a bad rap for that mistake, but it was an honest one. She honestly didn't try to make anyone sick. It was bad timing.

Poor planning, actually. She'd forgotten to defrost the chicken and thought it would be fine sitting out. Pesky bacteria. "You have to admit that it tasted good."

"It was delicious. But try not to kill off the rest of the family while you're at it."

She looked at the clock and saw it was a few minutes to five. If she headed out now, she could drop off a late dinner and offer her condolences. "Are you okay?" She imagined it was hard being Marybeth who dealt first-hand with every death in town. Then again, she got to snuggle newborn babies, and send brides down the aisle too. There was a balance to things, and Marybeth seemed to have a good one.

Charlotte turned off the lights, got her bag, and followed Marybeth to the door. She turned the sign to closed and locked up behind them. On the sidewalk, she gave her friend a hug, got in her car, and made her way home.

As she walked into the house, she stopped on the porch and glanced next door. It was dark, quiet, and lifeless, and her heart sank into the pit of her stomach.

She opened the door and moved past the overstuffed sofas and the table that held found objects like sea glass and starfish. She left her bag on the sofa table and went straight to the kitchen to put together her version of chicken and dumplings.

An hour later, she had a bubbling pot of homemade goodness that would fortify and fill. It might not fill the emptiness left by a death, but at least it would put something other than sorrow in their bellies.

As the sun set, she walked across the sand to her neighbor's door. With hands full, she used the toe of her shoe to knock. She waited and waited before she kicked at the door again. Preparing to turn back toward home, she pivoted and started for the steps as the door opened and a man stepped out.

"Can I help you?"

He looked rumpled and worn, but past the five o'clock shadow and his loosened tie, she could see that he had kind eyes, although red-rimmed and sad. His dark hair hung in clumps as if he'd been trying to pull it out at the ends.

"I'm Charlotte, your neighbor, and I'm so sorry for your loss." She glanced down at the pot in her hands. "I'm sure food is the last thing on your mind, but it's important to eat and nourish your body."

"You brought us food?" He stared at her.

"It's what we do here in Willow Bay." She lifted the pot and nodded to the oven mitts. "Despite what they tell you, they don't keep all the heat away. Before I blister, can I put this down somewhere?"

"Pardon my manners." He opened the door and nodded inside. "Kitchen is straight ahead."

Charlotte knew the layout because she'd been in the house a thousand times. It had changed owners over the years, but it had never changed. It was the same as it was the day it was built. Families had come and gone, but the bones of the home were the same.

She moved past the living room where an empty hospital bed sat dead center in the big bay window. On the couch sat a young woman who looked straight out of high school. Next to her was a little girl with long, brown hair.

"Hello Ivy, I'm Charlotte. Are you hungry? I brought over dinner."

Ivy lifted her head. "My tummy hurts."

"I imagine it does." Charlotte moved into the kitchen and set the pot on the stove. "Do you like chicken and dumplings?"

"I like everything," Ivy said. "My mom told me picky eaters don't get invited to many places, and I want to get invited everywhere and to everything."

"Your mom is smart." While she knew she was no longer with them, it didn't seem wise or necessary to talk about her mother in the past tense. Besides, Charlotte didn't believe that people actually left you. All science pointed to the fact that we are energy and energy never dies. "Would you like to set the table?" She looked at the man who leaned against the doorjamb. "Can I serve you?"

He narrowed his eyes. "Just so we're clear here, I'm not looking for a wife."

Charlotte's eyes widened. "All I'm offering is a meal. I think we're pretty clear. If you're looking for a wife or dessert, you're on your own."

Ivy picked up a bag of cookies—the same cookies Marybeth took from the box this morning. "We have these."

"You're very resourceful. How old are you?" She held up her hand with all her fingers splayed. "Wow, five?" Charlotte looked at the man. "Should I serve or go?"

The man pushed off the doorjamb. "I'm sorry. I'm Bastien, and this is my niece, Ivy, but you seem to already know her name. In the living room is Rachel. Ivy's helper."

Charlotte was relieved that he had help because he seemed overwhelmed. "It's good to have help. While I wish we had met under different circumstances, it's a pleasure to meet you, Bastien." Rather than wait for permission to serve, she opened the cupboards until she found bowls and set them on the counter. "How about one of you gets the silverware and the other the napkins?" She stepped back until she could see through the door to where Rachel sat on the couch. "Rachel, can you help us in here? I'm not sure what your dinner routine is, but if you can get drinks, that would be wonderful." She made a mental note to tell Marybeth that this family was going to need a lot of hospitality in the coming weeks.

They all did her bidding while she scooped up steaming bowls of chicken, gravy, vegetables, and dumplings.

Once they were seated around the table, she smiled. Her work here was done. "I'm next door if you need anything. I mean anything." She looked down at the meal and hoped they'd enjoy it. "While I'm not known for my cooking, I'm fairly certain none of you are headed for a case of salmonella poisoning or botulism, but if, for some reason, you feel unwell, Dr. Robinson is right next door."

"Should we be worried?" Bastien asked.

She thought about it for a second. She'd taken the meat out a day ago, or was it two days? She couldn't recall, but either way, it should be fine. "Nope. You're all good."

"Would you like to dine with us?" he asked.

Her stomach grumbled loudly, but she shook her head. "No. You should take time for your family." She backed out of the kitchen. "You know where to find me."

"Mommy would want you to stay," Ivy said. "She loved company."

Charlotte wanted to melt into the hardwood floor. She had lived next door and never once brought the woman a pie or a cookie or a glass of iced tea. How could she leave now?

"Thank you, I'll stay if you'd like." She walked to the cabinet, pulled another bowl down, filled it up, and took a seat across from Ivy. They ate in silence, and all Charlotte could think about was, what would happen to this little girl?

CHAPTER FOUR

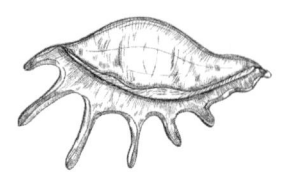

Bastien threw up twice last night. At first, he considered it might be Charlotte's meal, but no one else got sick. It had to be his nerves mixed with his incompetence. He knew nothing about kids. That was clear when he told Ivy it was time for bed at ten o'clock and she said her bedtime was at eight and had passed two hours ago. Then she told him she needed a bath and her teeth brushed and some kind of detangler put on her hair because it was Wednesday. What did he know about hair products? What did he know about detanglers? What did he know about raising a girl? What he knew was it was six in the morning. His mother was on her way and all there was to eat for breakfast in the house was a box of cereal and a questionable container of milk.

He looked at Ivy and Rachel, who sat at the dining room table. "Do you want to go to the grocery store or the diner?" Chloe wanted Ivy to have choices, so he figured it was better to give her some from the beginning.

"I want Charlotte."

He sighed. "She's not an option."

"But she's nice and she's pretty."

He agreed with both. She was nice, but he based that off of her bringing the meal. He'd heard that Southern hospitality was a thing but hadn't seen it in action until she showed up with dinner. As for her being pretty ... she was an attractive woman. He didn't know how to describe her, but angelic came to mind when he thought about her blonde hair and blue eyes. Maybe ethereal was more on point. Then again, he could be reading into her actions and not her looks because he hadn't thought about dinner. His gut had twisted and churned all afternoon and he hadn't considered eating. He should have thought about feeding Rachel and Ivy, but he hadn't. How in the world his sister thought he was a good fit for parenting was beyond him. One thing was certain: he'd need more help.

"Diner or grocery store?" he asked again.

"Diner," Rachel piped in. "Then there are no dirty dishes to clean." She turned to Ivy. "They have those chocolate chip pancakes you like."

"Diner," Ivy said as she slid from the chair and started for the door. "I'm starving."

"Diner it is." They grabbed Ivy's booster seat and piled into the rental car. The interior was sleek, with black leather and shiny chrome. The dashboard was lit like the flight deck of a 747. Why did everything have to be so complicated these days? With the push of a button, the car purred to life. "Does anyone know where the diner is?"

Rachel tapped on her phone and showed him the screen and then reached over and pushed a button on the steering wheel, saying, "Navigate to Cricket's Diner." A voice directed him from the beach to Main Street. He hadn't given the town a good look yet. Each time he arrived to see his sister, he went straight to the cottage, stayed a day or two, and left. But as he drove through the town, he could see why his sister loved it so much. It was warm and inviting, with its decorated windows enticing visitors to come in for a visit. He lucked out with a parking spot right in front of the diner and everyone piled out and headed inside.

The sweet aroma of sugar and warm butter hung in the air. It was almost a visible cloud. As he glanced around the restaurant decorated with chickens and roosters, he found an empty booth to the side.

Ivy slid in first and then Rachel beside her while he sat by himself on the bench across from them. The menus were stuffed into a metal holder against the wall.

"Who's going to pay me now?" Rachel asked.

"I am." He pulled out three menus and passed them out. There were a lot of things to consider, and he figured Rachel had a lot of questions. Ivy must too, but he didn't have any real answers. He was still living in his make-believe world, where his sister was going to beat cancer. He hadn't fully embraced his real world. The one where he was raising a five-year-old, and for all intents and purposes, Rachel, too. "How old are you?"

Rachel smiled. "I'm nineteen. This was supposed to be a summer gig, but I suppose you'll want to extend my contract?"

He nodded and opened the menu. "Look, Ivy, they do have chocolate chip pancakes."

Ivy's attention was on the rooster picture above them that read, *Do not make the chickens angry, they can be real peckers.*

"What's a pecker?"

The question was a shock. He wanted to laugh as well as crawl under the table. "You read?"

"She reads at a third-grade level," Rachel said with a

sense of pride, like she had something to do with it. Maybe she did.

"How long have you been working for Chloe?"

"Since June. I came down from Dallas to help."

"How did she find you?"

Rachel smiled. "Nannies R Us."

"Seriously?"

Rachel nodded. "I'm not kidding."

"What's a pecker?" Ivy demanded in a loud voice that turned heads.

The diner's bright fluorescent lights flickered, buzzed, and hummed overhead like he was under interrogation.

"Sorry for the wait." The waitress arrived at the table, smiled, and pulled out a pad of paper and a red pen that matched her high-top sneakers. She looked at the picture and then at Ivy. "A pecker is an angry or a hungry chicken." When she turned to him, she grinned. "What will you have?"

"Big breakfast, bacon, sourdough toast."

The woman scribbled his order down and turned to Ivy. "You're Ivy, right?"

Ivy looked at the picture. "Right now, I'm a pecker."

"Angry or hungry?"

Ivy stared at the woman whose name tag read Cricket. "I'm both."

Cricket leaned over and patted Ivy's hand. "I know, honey. I know about your mom, and I'm sorry." She stepped back and scribbled on the paper. "How about some chocolate chip pancakes with extra chip and whip?" She tapped her hair with the pen. "I think that's what you had the last time you came in, right?"

Ivy's little lip quivered, and a tear ran down her cheek.

"We came with mommy before she stayed in that bed by the window."

"Yes, you did. Chocolate milk, correct?"

Rachel raised her hand. "I'd like a veggie omelet with whole wheat toast."

Cricket pointed at Bastien. "You look like you could use coffee. I've got a special blend in the back. Do you want to try it?"

"Is it caffeinated?"

She smiled. "Sure as shit it is." She turned around and walked away.

"She said shit." Ivy giggled and covered her mouth. He didn't like her cussing, but he could handle that more easily than her tears.

"You said pecker," Rachel said.

"That's just a hungry chicken."

Bastien looked at Rachel and then at Ivy before he doubled over with laughter, his eyes crinkling and a loud, deep belly laugh echoing through the diner.

Cricket walked over and put a cup of coffee on the table. "This one is on the house, but the next cup is thirty bucks."

"That's some special brew," he said.

Cricket grinned, "It's the sh—"

"Got it," Bastien said.

Cricket turned to Ivy and winked. "Pancakes up in two."

Bastien picked up his cup and breathed in the rich, almost syrupy aroma with notes of chocolate, toffee, and just a hint of citrus. He usually doctored his coffee with lots of sugar and cream, but this cup deserved to be tasted as it was made.

He took a sip and let the liquid wrap around his tongue

like a velvety blanket. It was a different taste and sensation than he was used to, but he enjoyed it. At that price, he better savor it.

"How's the coffee?" Cricket showed up with her arms lined with plates. She set down Ivy's pancakes first. In whipped topping were two eyes and a crooked mouth that brought a smile to Ivy. Rachel got her veggie omelet, and he got his big breakfast with eggs, bacon, hash browns and toast.

"It's different, but it's good."

She fist-bumped the air. "I keep telling Charlotte it's good, but she won't even try it."

The mention of Charlotte made him feel warm inside. "We met Charlotte last night. She brought us dinner."

"That sounds like Charlotte. I imagine by tonight you won't have to worry about meals for weeks."

"Weeks? We don't need that many meals. We aren't staying."

Ivy dropped her fork. "We have to stay. This is where I live. I just started school."

Ivy wasn't like most kids. She was precocious and ferocious and far too smart for her own good. Chloe might have wanted her to have choices, but did that mean she got to choose everything? He wasn't used to living in a democracy. He was used to ruling his world. Something told him that everything was about to change.

They finished their meal, paid, and headed out. Rather than go straight to the car, Ivy skipped down the street. He thought she was heading to the candy shop on the corner, but she stopped in front of a store called Because You Said Yes. She pressed her nose against the glass and then squealed with delight before she raced inside.

"What the hell?" He ran a hand through his hair and

sighed. "Aren't you supposed to be with her? You're her nanny—it's your job!"

"I'm not her parent." Tears spilled down Rachel's cheeks. "I'm sad and under a lot of pressure. It's hard to focus when I don't know what's going to happen next."

"We're all confused. You're not the only one who's sad. That was my sister. I'm sad too, but we have to move forward, and Ivy needs consistency."

"Is that why you're moving her to who knows where? That doesn't sound stable."

He wasn't going to stand there and argue with a teenager, so he moved past her and into the shop where he found Ivy talking to Charlotte. They were discussing types of paper while Charlotte took several sheets of what looked like fancy and expensive linen paper and put them into a bag.

"I think your mother would love these."

"Hey bug, you can't take off like that." Bastien walked to the counter and tugged one of Ivy's long locks before pulling out his wallet. "What do I owe you for the paper?"

Charlotte's face lit up with a smile, and he had a vision of an angel. "No charge," she said. "Ivy intends to write her mom a letter and some pretty paper will make it perfect."

He nodded in agreement.

"She told me you ate at the diner. Was it good?" Charlotte asked.

"Just a coffee and breakfast," he replied.

Charlotte produced a tissue from a nearby box and wiped the chocolate from Ivy's mouth. "Ah, and chocolate!" She spun around, flicking the tissue into a bin. "I hope Cricket didn't get you to try her special brew."

"What do you mean?" he said, unable to figure out what was going on.

"Did you drink it?"

He glanced away, trying his best to avoid her gaze. "I'm not sure I want to answer that."

"You already did," she chuckled, reaching up to cover her mouth in an attempt to contain her laughter.

"Excuse me?"

Turning to him, she shared a mischievous grin. "Kopi Luwak, or civet coffee. Just search for it." She grabbed Ivy by the hand and led her behind the counter. "How about some glitter? I'm pretty sure I have some in my office!"

Bastien took out his phone and typed in "civet coffee." But when he saw that the beverage he had just consumed came from coffee beans that had been eaten, digested, and excreted by an animal resembling a cross between a raccoon and a ferret, he couldn't help himself from grimacing in disgust—he had just ingested a liquid litter box!

As Charlotte and Ivy came back from her office, he fled to the back room with one hand clasped over his mouth, raging nausea threatening to take away any semblance of composure that he had left. "Where's the bathroom?" he called out.

"First door on the right," Charlotte answered.

When he came out of the bathroom pale-faced, he walked to where Charlotte and Ivy sat at a big table writing letters.

"You feeling alright?"

He nodded. "I just want to be clear. I was sick last night, and I can't rule out your food." His stomach tightened as her angelic smile lit up her face.

"My money is on the cat feces."

"What's feces?" Ivy asked.

Charlotte looked at him as if to ask him if he wanted to

explain, and he didn't want to touch this subject with a ten-foot-pole.

"You started it. You explain it to her. I have nothing left in me—literally."

Charlotte looked at Ivy. "Cat faces, honey. Aren't cats adorable?" She looked over her shoulder and winked. "Bastien, if you need to do other stuff, I'm happy to take Ivy home once the shop closes. My driving record is better than my cooking and everyone in town can vouch for my trustworthiness. It's up to you and Ivy, of course, but I'm happy to help. Besides, it's not like anyone is busting down my door to plan a wedding."

He spun around in surprise. "This is a wedding store?"

"Because You Said Yes," she replied. "Nothing is impossible—all you need to do is ask for it."

"Is that true? Can you get whatever anyone wants?"

She grabbed a golden pen and handed it to Ivy. "What do you want?"

CHAPTER FIVE

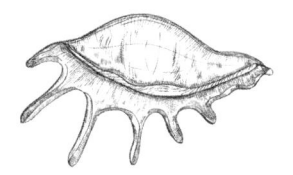

Charlotte waited for him to respond.

"Right now, I need a good night's sleep," Bastien said. "But I'd settle for anything that could calm my nerves."

"That's something I can help with." Charlotte grabbed a few things from the shelf beside her and brought them to the counter. She carefully placed a teapot, cup, saucer, and a small honey jar on the glass. "This is Cricket's honey. She raises the bees herself. She claims it's the elixir of the gods and has everyone believing it will cure everything from wrinkles to bad moods." Charlotte plugged in the instant teapot, and the water churned to a boil. "I figure if we mix my tea with Cricket's honey, we've got a recipe for success."

Bastien looked up at Charlotte. "I would love some tea. What kind is it?"

Charlotte smiled as she opened the jar so he could smell it. "It's my blend of chamomile, lavender, honeybush, jasmine, and peppermint, blended with a hint of lemon and ginger. It should help you relax and hopefully get your mind off things for a while."

He brought the jar to his nose, breathed in the mixture,

and then nodded before handing it back to her. "Smells great." He sighed. "My sister Chloe always loved tea."

"It's therapeutic." She measured the herbs into a basket and placed it in a cup before covering it with boiling water. "We'll let it steep for a few minutes."

Charlotte helped Ivy with her letter while Bastien walked around her shop. She watched him for a moment before speaking again. "Like I said, if you've got things to do, I can keep an eye on Ivy. I imagine you've got lots of planning." She glanced down at Ivy and whispered, "You know, arrangements and stuff."

"Chloe made all her arrangements. I have to pick up my mother, who's arriving in Galveston, but we'll do that together. No one should face Annette Richmond alone." He turned to Ivy. "Grandma is coming today."

Ivy frowned. "She doesn't like to be called Grandma."

He cocked his head to the side. "What do you call her?"

"Mee-maw."

"And she likes that?"

Ivy shrugged. "I don't think she likes anything, even me."

Charlotte felt her heart break. She wanted to put her arms around Ivy and tell her that Mee-maw must love her. After all, she was on her way. But she knew that wouldn't be the right thing to do in this situation. She didn't know the family or its dynamics.

Instead, Charlotte cleared her throat and offered a comforting smile. "I'm sure she's looking forward to seeing you," she said reassuringly.

Ivy dipped her chin before turning her gaze towards Bastien. He was standing in the corner of the room, silently watching their exchange. The corners of his mouth turned down, and his eyes were dark like the sky on a cloudless night. He hadn't said anything throughout the entire exchange, but Charlotte could see the emotion playing on his face.

He cleared his throat before speaking up. "We should probably get going," he mumbled as he stepped forward and placed a gentle hand on Ivy's shoulder.

Charlotte nodded as she reached for the cup of tea on the counter. She handed it to Bastien. "Here," she said softly, "Drink this first. It might help."

Bastien accepted the cup of tea from Charlotte, taking a small sip before setting it back down. He looked at Ivy, and all Charlotte could see was love and sadness in his eyes. He knelt, so he was at eye level with her, and said, "Ivy, we have to go now. Mee-maw's flight arrives soon, and she needs us to pick her up."

Ivy nodded sadly and wrapped her arms around Bastien's neck for a hug before he stood up. He gave Charlotte a grateful look, and she smiled back in understanding before walking over and giving him a reassuring pat on the shoulder."Everything will be okay," she murmured before taking a step back. Bastien glanced around the store before turning to leave with Ivy. As they stepped from the counter, Charlotte whispered, "Good luck."

Charlotte watched as the two figures disappeared around the corner, and a wave of sadness rushed over her. Then she noticed Ivy had left her letter. She set it aside and cleaned up the table. She'd bring Ivy's letter over after she closed up shop for the day.

Cricket opened the door with her free hand, balancing two steaming cups of coffee in the other. The smell of freshly brewed coffee quickly filled the shop.

"You better not be bringing me a cup of your special brew," Charlotte said with a laugh.

Cricket's eyes rolled upwards, and the corner of her mouth twitched into a sly smile. "Your neighbor loved it," she said as she carefully set one cup on the counter. "You can't judge something until you've tasted it."

Charlotte shook her head and stared at the cup. "My neighbor threw it up along with his breakfast shortly after he visited."

Cricket chuckled. "I bet you told him I gave him cat shit," she replied knowingly.

Charlotte couldn't help but laugh at her friend's comment. "Well, you did," she said before taking a sip from the cup Cricket had handed her. The smell of chicory filled her nose and caused her to sigh in pleasure and relief.

"It's not like they raid litter boxes. It's the undigested beans they find in the wild, and they've been treated to be safe," Cricket said. "That poor man didn't get sick from my coffee but from stress. Rumor has it Chloe asked him to raise Ivy."

Charlotte's jaw dropped. "She wants him to raise Ivy?"

Cricket shrugged. "Yeah. I guess Chloe was close to Bastien, and Ivy loves him, so Chloe thought it would be best if he could take care of her."

Charlotte shook her head in disbelief. She knew little about Bastien, but he appeared out of his element. But he also seemed like the kind of person who would do anything for Ivy. "It must be hard for him," she said, thinking about the heartbreaking situation of losing a sister and gaining a child.

"It would be difficult for anyone," Cricket said.

Charlotte had little experience with children, but at least she'd been around them. She had babysat before. But she also knew that having a child full-time was more than just childcare; it was parenting an individual and taking on all the responsibilities that came with it. Taking care of Ivy would be a massive undertaking for Bastien.

"It's amazing," Cricket said in admiration, "that he's willing to take on such responsibility even though he has no idea what he's doing."

Charlotte nodded in agreement. "I think he loves her enough to make it work," she said.

Cricket gave Charlotte a reassuring smile and picked up her cup. "Let's hope so," she said as they clinked their coffees together.

After being steeped in silence for several moments, Charlotte looked up at Cricket and sighed heavily. "Do you think just anyone can raise a child?" she asked as she stared out into the street from behind the counter.

Cricket seemed to ponder her question before answering. "I believe anyone can if they have the love and support needed to succeed."

"That's the thing. I think he is alone. He and Ivy are on their way to pick up his mother, but I get the feeling they aren't close. Ivy doesn't think her grandmother likes her." Charlotte lifted her hands in the air. "Who wouldn't love that little girl to pieces?" Charlotte gave her friend a small smile and then looked back down at the cup of coffee she had been sipping. She felt terrible for Bastien and wished there was something more she could do to help. "Do you know anything about his mother?"

Cricket shook her head. "Not much," she said. "The rumor mill says she's from Atlanta, but that's all I know. Why would Chloe want Bastien to raise her daughter and not her mother?"

"Maybe they were estranged?"

"Or the mom's deranged."

Charlotte frowned. She didn't know how a single man was supposed to raise a child without family members' help or support. "That poor man," she murmured as she shook her head.

Cricket nodded in agreement, her face mirroring Charlotte's sympathetic expression. "Is there anything we can do?" she asked, her voice thoughtful and concerned.

Charlotte sighed and looked up at Cricket thoughtfully. She knew Cricket was invested in the townsfolk's welfare, and Bastien was now part of this town.

"I don't think there is anything we can do right now," Charlotte said after a few moments of silence, her voice heavy with regret. "But I think it would be nice if we could check in on him every once in a while, and make sure he's okay."

Cricket nodded, though lines of worry still lingered on her forehead. She knew that while they couldn't solve all of Bastien's problems, they could at least provide moral support when needed. "I agree," she said. "With you being next door, you're in the best position to do that."

Charlotte drained the last dregs of her coffee cup and nodded in agreement. She knew if Bastien needed anything, she could easily be there for him.

"That's true," Charlotte said after a moment of thought. "I'll keep an eye on him and ensure he has what he needs." She smiled warmly at Cricket and patted her hand reassuringly. "You don't have to worry about Bastien. I'll take care of him."

Cricket smiled back at Charlotte. "I'm glad you're here," she said, her expression full of relief. "And I know Bastien will appreciate it too." She paused for a moment before continuing, her voice serious now. "Just remember, though, that he might not be open to help or advice right away—he'll need time to adjust."

She and Bastien seemed to be kindred spirits because they both had to build something from nothing. He was building a family, and she a future.

"My break is over," Cricket said as she hugged Charlotte. "I have to go."

"I'll see you soon." Charlotte walked her to the door. As Cricket walked out, the postman walked in and handed her the mail.

Charlotte stared at the pile of envelopes in her hand, and a feeling of dread washed over her. She knew that some of those letters would contain bills for supplies and services she had used for her business, but the weight of them felt like more than she could handle.

She took them back to the table where she and Ivy had decorated the letter and went through them individually. Her heart sank into the pit of her stomach with each passing letter. The amount she owed far exceeded her current funds. How was she going to make money to pay all those bills?

CHAPTER SIX

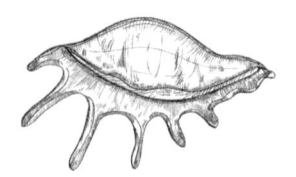

As Bastien exited the shop, he noticed Rachel perched on a wooden bench out front. She had her hands folded in her lap and her head bowed, deep in thought. "You ready?"

She slowly raised her head, her eyes meeting his. Her mouth became a thin line. "As I'll ever be," she said in a low voice, full of resignation.

They headed over to the SUV.

"I want to sit in the front," Ivy pleaded.

He glanced over at Rachel as if expecting her to say something, but she just sighed and got in the back seat.

He scratched the back of his neck and glanced around before gazing down at the hopeful face of his niece. He knew the rules, knew he was breaking them, but he couldn't find the words to refuse her. "Okay," he said with a sigh, "you can ride shotgun, but just this time."

Ivy cheered and clapped her hands. He shifted her booster to the front seat and helped her buckle up to make sure she was secure, then went around and got into the driver's seat.

A press of the ignition button brought the car to a murmuring start. Too bad everything didn't run so smoothly or quietly. They headed down Main Street, making their way to the highway that would take them to Galveston.

"So, what's the game plan?" Rachel questioned.

"Right now, I plan to pick up my mom from the airport. I have nothing else planned after that. I'm just taking it one moment at a time." He looked up at Rachel in the rearview mirror. "And what about you? What's in store for you?" He wanted to know if she was considering extending their agreement. "Will you stay as Ivy's helper?"

"Can I let you know shortly?"

"Of course." He hadn't considered how much Chloe's death could have affected her. She had to be as saddened by it as anyone else. "I'm sorry for your loss, too." She nodded silently in response before turning away and leaning against the car door.

The further they got from Willow Bay, the more his mind drifted to the conversation he'd had with Chloe the day she died—was that only yesterday? She looked frail and tired, but her eyes were sharp and wise. "There is no other choice. Promise me, Bastien," she had said. "If you do nothing else for me, promise me you'll raise Ivy." He had promised Chloe he'd watch over Ivy, but it was hard to know how to be a good father figure when he had never had one.

He kept his eyes on the road and his thoughts on that promise. He had to be strong for Ivy, no matter what happened. He wanted her to have the childhood he and Chloe never had. He wanted Ivy to be happy and feel appreciated and loved.

Even if it was the scariest thing he had ever done, he was determined to be a good guardian for Ivy. He reached over and squeezed her little hand. He knew that as long as he kept this promise to Chloe, everything would work out in the end, and he prayed it would.

His phone rang, and his mother's name came on the screen. Bastien glanced at the car's dashboard, over the bright display of the clock. His eyes widened as he read the time—it was ten minutes before his mother was due to arrive. He swallowed hard, lifting the phone to his ear, and speaking into it with a strained voice. "Hey, Mom," he said, with an edge of apprehension. "Did you get here early?"

A deep exhale left his mother's lips. "I did," she said, her voice laden with frustration. "But you're not here. I've always told you that early was on time and on time was late."

With a clenched jaw, he spoke. "Mom, now isn't the time. I'm dealing with a lot." He reached over and squeezed Ivy's hand to reassure her that everything would be alright.

"You're dealing with a lot? My daughter died, and she didn't even let me say goodbye." Her voice quivered with unspoken emotion. Her words had a tremor of pain and grief, yet her tone was resolute. It was a reminder that no matter what situation arose, Annette Richmond was a force to be reckoned with, and she refused to be swayed by excuses or denials.

"We're rounding the corner to the terminal. I'll pick you up there." He hung up and glanced at Ivy. He hadn't noticed it when they left that morning, but now, as he scanned her from head to toe, he realized her ensemble was an eyesore. Her dress was purple and baggy. Her sweater was two sizes too big and a deep shade of brown, and her socks were mismatched—one pink, one blue. He shuddered at the thought of how she must have looked to a passerby, like she had just dressed herself from a lost and found bin at school.

He looked over his shoulder. "Did you pick that outfit for her?"

Rachel laughed. "No, Ivy knows what she likes, and Chloe wanted her to have—"

"Choices." He understood the concept of "choices," although he doubted his mother would. As children, they were dressed by stylists. There was no sin greater than embarrassing their mother.

"Ivy, darling. As soon as we pull up to the curb, you'll have to get into the back seat with Rachel."

"Okay, Uncle Bast," she said sweetly.

When they rounded the bend, his mother stood there with an air of superiority, tapping her foot impatiently. She was dressed in a sharp black pantsuit that made her look like she was attending a boardroom meeting, rather than visiting her grief-stricken family. Her Louis Vuitton luggage was lined up beside her, three large pieces of it—how long did she plan on staying? He parked the car, got out, and walked to the passenger door.

"Hello, Mother," he said, embracing her in a stiff hug.

Annette Richmond stepped back and frowned at him. "You should have been here earlier."

"I apologize." He opened Ivy's door.

Mom looked past him towards Ivy, who had climbed out of the car. Her eyes widened in surprise as she took in the mismatched outfit.

"Who dressed you today?" Annette asked, her voice showing every ounce of shock and disapproval.

Bastien swiftly reached for Ivy's hand and explained, "She wanted to dress herself this morning."

"Allowing a kid in her closet is like letting a fox in the chicken coop. It's a pure disaster," Annette said.

He assisted Ivy as she sat in the back and kissed her on the cheek, whispering, "You look beautiful, little ladybug."

Annette lifted an eyebrow but thankfully did not comment any further. Instead, she shifted her attention to her bags.

"Be careful with the smaller bag. It has my makeup and valuables."

Bastien couldn't help but chuckle. "Does it take an entire makeup suitcase to make you presentable?"

"I have jewelry too."

He grabbed the smaller bag, careful not to disturb the precious cargo inside, and loaded it into the back of their SUV before the others, then headed back to the driver's side.

"It better be the Hope Diamond with how much that weighed."

"It's not easy being a woman. We aren't allowed to age. If we do, we find ourselves alone."

Under his breath, he said, "Or at the pool with Francois." He pulled into traffic.

"What was that?"

"I said, how long are you staying?"

"A few days. Just long enough to bury Chloe and pack up Ivy to return to Atlanta."

He stepped on the brake, and the car behind them honked in protest. "Ivy is staying with me."

Bastien's hands clenched the steering wheel, his knuckles turning white from the pressure of his grip. He glanced briefly at his mother, who was sitting stiffly in the passenger seat. Her pursed lips and tightly crossed arms said everything; he could feel the heat of her disapproval radiating from her like a campfire.

"Don't be absurd," she said sharply. "What are you going to do with a five-year-old baby?"

"I'm not a baby," Ivy protested quietly.

Annette held up her hand to the back seat. "Children are supposed to be seen and not heard."

"And that's why Chloe made me promise to raise her," Bastien said. "She doesn't want Ivy silenced."

Annette scoffed but remained quiet.

The atmosphere in the car was oppressive as they drove until, finally, Bastien spoke up again. "Let's not do this here."

His mother rolled her eyes but kept quiet, allowing him some small victory in this battle of wills between them.

Bastien glanced into the rearview mirror at Ivy, who was looking at him. He smiled reassuringly at her before refocusing his gaze towards their destination: home–wherever that may be for the time being.

"Mee-maw looks like a pecker."

Rachel laughed and then snorted.

He did his best not to join her in laughing.

"I'm a what?" His mother glared at him. "Is that the language you're teaching my granddaughter?"

"She's being observant." He had to admit that Ivy was right. With her pinched lips and angry eyes, his mother resembled the angry chicken in the picture in the diner. "You look like a poster she saw recently."

His mother spun around to face the back seat, eyeing Rachel. "Isn't she young for you?" An odd, guttural noise vibrated in the air. It was unrefined and came as a shock. "You're just like your father."

"That's Ivy's nanny, mother. Rachel, meet Annette

Richmond. Mom, meet Rachel, and before you ask, she's nineteen, and this was a summer gig."

"What was wrong with Chloe?"

"Cancer," Ivy said with the same authority his mother had used earlier. "She died of cancer, but we had a day of crying, and Mommy didn't want any tears after that."

His mother's jaw dropped. "Aren't you sad?"

Ivy nodded. "I'm allowed to be sad, but it's okay because Uncle Bast and I are going to take care of each other."

"You're coming to Atlanta with Mee-maw, where we'll get you a new wardrobe, and I'll put you into a lovely private school where you'll get the best education." She tapped her chin. "We'll try Baylor when she reaches sixth grade for boarding."

Bastien quickly sped up his car, maneuvering through the streets until he could turn around and head back to the airport.

"Where do you think you're going?" his mother questioned.

"Back to the airport. I'm not letting you continue talking about Ivy as if she's not here and has no choices—and I'm sure as hell not allowing you to send Ivy away to boarding school. There's no better way to show someone that you love and care about them than to keep them close."

"But these are great schools."

"Maybe, but not for Ivy, and certainly not something to decide before she's even started first grade," he answered firmly. "She already lost her mother," he whispered. "I will not allow her to feel like she doesn't matter to the rest of us." Was this how a parent felt—possessive and protective? He'd questioned his sister's decision to ask him to raise Ivy, but now he understood. He was Ivy's only chance at a normal upbringing. He drove straight to the departure terminal and pulled to the curb.

"Bastien Alexander Richmond. What do you think you're doing?" his mother asked.

"I'm dropping you off. If you're not bringing something positive into our lives, then you have no place in our lives." He parked the car and got out, going straight to the back to retrieve her luggage, which he set on the curb. He opened her door and helped her out.

"But what about Chloe's service?"

"It's tomorrow at the church at eleven o'clock."

"How will I know which church?" She smoothed out the crinkles in the black fabric of her pantsuit.

"I'm told you can't miss it. It's the white building with a cross on the steeple."

"Where will I stay?"

"You'll figure it out. You always do." He kissed her cheek and jogged to the driver's side of the car. Once inside, he turned to Ivy. "Shall we go back to the cottage on the beach?"

"And Charlotte?" Ivy asked.

"And Charlotte," Bastien replied, a smile forming on his lips for no clear reason.

CHAPTER SEVEN

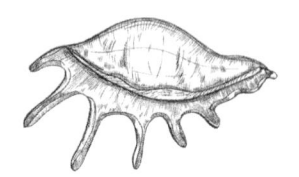

At five o'clock, Charlotte slowly moved around the store, surveying the merchandise one last time before turning off the lights. Her stomach flipped at the sight of the pile of bills sitting on the counter—she would have to prioritize them tonight, but for now she picked them up and tucked them into her bag.

Ivy's letter, which she'd lovingly embellished with glitter and stars, drew her attention. She ran her fingers over the paper, feeling the heartfelt message inside, before slipping it into her bag next to the pile of bills. She reminded herself that if a five-year-old could find joy writing a letter to her deceased mom, nothing in Charlotte's life was awful. With that, she took a deep breath and stepped out of the store. The golden light from the setting sun glowed orange around her, painting a beautiful masterpiece stretching from one side of town to the other.

For a moment, Charlotte felt herself drift away from her worries and concerns—all that mattered at this moment was the beauty of nature surrounding her. Sensing that only a few precious moments were left before dusk settled in and brought a chill, she drew in one last deep breath and allowed herself a moment of peace before heading home for the night. She smiled, grateful for these moments of beauty and contentment that were part of the charm to living in Willow Bay.

She climbed into her car and headed toward her little bungalow on the beach. As she pulled into her driveway, the familiar sight of her home filled her with warmth. It had been in her family for over a hundred years. Her grandfather worked on the docks and won the land in a poker game. They weren't rich like the Kesslers or the Browns, but they always had enough. That was the message her Grandma Ida was famous for. You never needed more than enough. Her Grandpa Sam drilled in the idea that the harder one worked, the luckier one got, but Charlotte was pretty sure her grandfather was a card shark. Charlotte had never won a single game of anything in all the years she'd spent with him.

She parked the car and stepped out, glancing next door to see the SUV. Ivy and Bastien had safely made it back from the airport. She had to deliver Ivy's letter but decided to gussy up first. She told herself it was because she was meeting Ivy's grandmother, but deep down, she knew she wanted to look her best for her handsome neighbor.

Charlotte hurried to her bedroom, where she chose three outfits. She held up the navy-blue dress with the white sweetheart collar and shook her head. She wasn't heading to church. She picked up the pantsuit and stepped in front of the mirror, holding it in front of her. While it was nice, it looked like she was interviewing for a secretarial position. In fact, the last time she wore the outfit was for an interview to be the mayor's administrative assistant. She was confident she could assist him any way he needed. She could pull together a luncheon without a hitch, and she had all the connections to get him a reservation anywhere he wanted to dine. The problem was, he wanted her to type seventy-five words per minute. Who knew that was still a thing? She hadn't seen an actual typewriter since she went to finishing school with Emmaline. They snuck out of typing class most days to meet with the boys from a nearby boarding school. The only reason she passed the class was because Marybeth assisted in the office and changed their grade to a C-. But that was before she met the preacher, and honesty and integrity outweighed friendship and loyalty. She tossed the pantsuit aside and looked at the third outfit. It was a pair of clam diggers and a pretty pink boat neck sweater she paired with white Keds. It was youthful and comfortable and something she would have worn at home.

She changed into the clothes and headed to the bathroom. If she was playing down her outfit, she'd up her makeup game. Being a fair-skinned blonde often made her look washed out. Cricket once told her she was see-through. No Southern woman worth her salt wanted to be that. She was no wallflower. She applied an extra coat of mascara, touched up her foundation and pinked her cheeks before applying her favorite lipstick, called Love Potion. She wasn't looking for love. She was the girl that rarely got past the test drive or maybe she just preferred the honeymoon phase to the everything-after part. She thought it funny that Bastien warned her he was not looking for a wife. While she was slightly jealous of her blissfully married friends, she wasn't looking, either. The only good thing about marriage was the wedding and if she could get her business to take off, she'd experience plenty of those.

Taking a few calming breaths, Charlotte picked up Ivy's letter and willed herself into action. She started towards the house. It was a cute little cottage with whitewashed siding and navy-blue shutters. The porch had a rocking chair and a pot of flowers desperately in need of water. As she knocked on the door, butterflies fluttered furiously in her stomach. What in the world? Was it the death, seeing the sorrow in Ivy's eyes, or Bastien? The door opened and there he was—tall, handsome, and even more captivating than she remembered. She felt her face flush instantly and knew exactly where that fluttery feeling came from.

"Charlotte," he said with a smile.

"Sorry to bother you. I know you have a lot going on, but Ivy left her letter in the store, and I wanted her to have it for the service tomorrow." She thrust the bedazzled letter forward, and he took it from her.

He gestured for her to enter. "It's no bother at all. We were just about to have pizza. Will you join us?"

She was hesitant to intrude on their meal, but her traitorous stomach let loose a loud growl. She clasped her hands over her belly to still the sound. "I'm sorry," she whispered. "I skipped lunch."

"It would be a sin to refuse Carlo's Pizza!" He waved her in. "Pull up a chair and stay for dinner."

"No, I shouldn't." She glanced past him to the kitchen and saw Ivy and Rachel sitting at the table; an unopened box of pizza sat between them.

"I think your stomach already said yes!"

"Did you say Carlo's?" She stepped inside, and Bastien closed the door. She lifted her nose into the air and breathed in the scent of freshly cooked dough, melted cheese, and spicy pepperoni. "Extra cheese?" she asked.

"And pepperoni."

"I'm in." She walked into the kitchen, expecting to find Ivy's grandmother tucked into the corner chair, but there were only the two girls.

Ivy launched herself out of the chair and threw herself into Charlotte's arms. "I missed you." She squeezed Charlotte's neck and kissed her cheek. "I forgot my letter."

"This letter?" Bastien held up the envelope before setting it on the kitchen counter.

"Thank you," Ivy said. "Are you staying for pizza?"

"I am."

"Rachel," Ivy yelled. "Charlotte's stayin' for pizza."

Rachel sighed. "I'll alert the media."

Bastien opened the box and served everyone a slice before he took the seat across from Charlotte. The last time she'd seen him, he was wearing a suit, but tonight he was dressed in jeans and a Henley. Why hadn't she noticed how hot he was before? Probably because all the blood drained from her brain when she saw him. What was the deal with Bastien?

"I thought you were picking up your mother."

"I did, and five minutes in the car was too much, so I turned around and dropped her back at the airport."

"That was a quick trip."

"Oh, she didn't leave. I'm sure she found a way back to town. One thing is certain, my mother will not go away easily."

"Mommy said that Mee-maw's as cuddly as a hornet."

"A hornet, huh?" She turned to face Bastien. "Out of the mouths of babes."

"And she's being kind."

"Wow."

They gobbled their first piece of pizza and were on their

second when Ivy laid the remaining crust down. "Can Rachel and I look for seashells?"

"Sure."

Charlotte was suddenly alone with Bastien. "She seems to be handling all of this okay."

He rubbed the scruff on his face and cocked his head to the right. "My sister did a wonderful job of preparing her. While I know she's sad and feels the loss, Chloe told her that even though she wasn't here to talk to and touch that she was everywhere, like in the seashells and the wind. Ivy likes that thought."

"I believe the same. We're energy, and energy never goes away; it just goes somewhere else." She finished the last of her pizza and pushed the plate aside. "You want to talk about what happened with your mom?"

He chuckled. "That would take a lifetime."

"I've got an hour or so." She didn't mind being an ear to Bastien. It was almost like recompense for not being a friend to his sister. "You don't seem like a man who'd go all the way to Galveston to pick up his mom, only to abandon her there."

"She plans to send Ivy to boarding school."

Charlotte frowned. "I thought Chloe wanted you to take care of her." She realized she shouldn't have known that information, so she shrugged. "Small town news travels fast."

"That is what Chloe wanted, but am I the right choice? I feel like right now, I'm the lesser of two evils."

She reached across the table and touched his arm. "That makes you the right choice, then."

"I live in New York City, and Ivy has informed me she's not moving."

Charlotte's heart raced. "You're leaving? Too much change can be damaging. She's already lost her mother. Do you think a big move is wise?"

He sighed. "But New York is where I work. It's what I do."

She thought about that for a moment. "It's what you used to do. You are no longer what you thought you were if you decide to raise Ivy. Children have a way of redefining you."

"Do you have children?"

She shook her head. "No kids. No husband." She immediately recalled his statement about not looking for a wife. "And I'm not looking." Realizing that might have sounded as abrupt as his declaration, she added, "A wise columnist once wrote—anyone looking for a husband hasn't had one."

He chuckled. "Duly noted." He closed the pizza box and gathered the plates. "Will you come to the service tomorrow?"

She shook her head. "I didn't know your sister."

He dumped the trash in the can and put the plates in the sink. "She would have liked you."

"You think?"

"I know, and it would mean so much to Ivy to have a friendly face." He stared at her for a moment. "And to me."

"Then I'll be there." She was the boss and could make her own hours. Closing for a funeral was a legitimate reason to be absent for a brief spell.

"Shall we check on the girls?" he asked.

"That seems sensible. Rachel doesn't seem focused, and even though Ivy appears to be quite mature for her five years, it's better to be safe than sorry."

They easily found the two girls picking up shells at the shoreline.

"They look unharmed, so I'll let you get back to managing them. Thanks for the pizza."

"It was my pleasure," he said, shocking her with an unexpected hug and making her heart skip a beat. She left feeling warmth in her soul and a spring in her step.

CHAPTER EIGHT

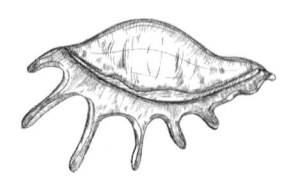

As the sun crested the horizon, Bastien rose from his unsettled slumber and peeked in on Ivy, who was cozied up against her beloved teddy bear.

Today was Chloe's funeral, and with a heavy heart, he took a morning jog down the beach. While he was hopeful the fresh salty air would help him clear his head, he passed by house after house, noticing that his emotions were becoming more tangled with every step.

His entire life had turned on a dime. Last week he was knee-deep in the hustle and bustle of moneymaking in New York City, and now he was in the sleepy town of Willow Bay, breathing in the fresh, salty air. He had a five-year-old child to care for, his sister was gone, and his mother was as cantankerous as an angry weasel. In hindsight, abandoning her at the side of the road wasn't his best decision—he knew she wouldn't be pleased with that—but his patience had been exhausted.

He was almost home when a wave of recognition washed over him. Her blonde hair blew in the breeze, catching the sun, and despite his fatigue and the throbbing in his legs, he picked up his pace and jogged towards her. His heart raced as he approached, and the worries and stresses of his day melted away as soon as he saw her angel eyes.

"You're up early," Charlotte said, holding a cup of coffee and smiling. "Would you like a cup?"

"Is it feline feces-free?" He scrunched his nose.

"It's one hundred percent Colombian and cat poop-free." She chuckled. "I can't believe you drank that coffee."

He shrugged. "I didn't ask enough questions, and it's not something you'd expect in a quiet little town. I just wanted to know if it had caffeine in it."

"Was it awful?"

He rocked his head back and forth as if debating. "Surprisingly, no. I liked it until I found out what was actually in it."

Charlotte hung her head. "I'm sorry."

"You can make it up to me by getting me a cup of your coffee," he said.

"Come on in." She waved him towards her house. His eyes fell on the small cottage, no bigger or grander than his sister's place. Instead of white-washed wood, Charlotte's place was a faded yellow, just a shade lighter than butter, and the shutters were white with black metal accents.

As she opened the door, Bastien noticed a cozy overstuffed sofa and a table full of driftwood and sea glass.

"Do you still collect this stuff?" he asked. He knew lots of people gathered these types of treasures. A jar half-filled with glass was on his sister's kitchen counter. He couldn't tell if it was Chloe's, Ivy's, or Rachel's.

"I used to. It was like searching for buried treasure to

me. It felt like I had struck gold when I found something special."

He held up a piece of green glass, its surface reflecting the afternoon light. "Do you have a favorite?" he asked.

She paused and looked around the room, her eyes lingering on a small piece of red glass on the tabletop. She picked it up and turned it over in her hands, its smooth facets glinting in the light. "This is my favorite," she said softly, "because you rarely see red glass. I found it when I was twelve and was convinced it was a ruby." She offered it to him, and he accepted, bringing it to his eyes to examine it against the light.

He tried to guess what it used to be before it was reduced to little more than a gleaming fragment in his hands. "Did you ever figure out what it was from?"

She shrugged, a smile playing on her lips. "There used to be something called Red Rum, but that's rare now. And Chanel No 5 had a limited-edition red bottle of their perfume at one point. I still like to think it's a ruby, but who knows?"

"I guess it remains a mystery."

"Or a ruby... You didn't come here to examine my knick-knacks. You came for coffee." She proceeded into the kitchen, which was like his sister's. Charlotte's, however, had nicer appliances and furniture.

"Nice oven." He wasn't much of a cook, but he knew high quality when he saw it and that Wolf range was the best of the best.

"My mom loved cooking," Charlotte said.

"Is she still living?"

"No, she passed away a couple of years ago." She turned her back, raised herself on her toes to reach a coffee mug, and filled it to just under the brim. "My father died the year before her. My dad passed away from the flu, but I think my mother died from a broken heart."

"That's terribly sad," he said.

"Some people are so devoted that if their partner dies, they feel like there's no purpose for them." She handed him the cup. "Do you need cream or sugar?"

"Both, please."

She moved to the refrigerator and pulled out a carton of half and half and then went to the small table and slid the sugar bowl toward him. "Help yourself."

She reached for a spoon in a nearby drawer and passed it to him. As he scooped a heaping teaspoon of sugar into his cup, his eyes drifted to the stack of bills on the table, and when she noticed him looking, she grabbed them and put them in a drawer.

"Sorry, I'm normally tidier."

He took a sip of his coffee and smiled. "Life is sometimes messy."

"It sure can be. Speaking of life, what's your plan?" She pulled out a chair and took a seat.

He took the empty seat next to her. "I'm not sure." He rolled his head and listened to his vertebrae pop. "I was here for a visit." He pinched the bridge of his nose. "The truth is, I came here to check in on Chloe. I never expected her to die—she had such fight and determination. I was sure she could beat cancer."

"I'm sure she didn't want to leave, but sometimes we don't have a choice."

"True. This whole trip seems to circle that one word—choice."

Her eyes grew wide. "How so?"

"It's why Chloe wants me to raise Ivy."

"She seems fond of you." Charlotte sipped her coffee and set it down. "Is that what you want?"

He shrugged. "It doesn't matter what I want; I made a promise, and I have to keep it."

Charlotte sipped her coffee before asking, "Are you staying, then?"

He shook his head. "I have a lot of stuff to take care of in New York."

"Are you going to bring Ivy back with you?"

He ran his hands through his hair. "That's part of the issue. I turned right around when my mom started talking about sending Ivy to private school and boarding school yesterday, but the truth is, if she comes to live with me in New York, she'll get the same thing—private education and a nanny."

Charlotte bit her lower lip, and he could sense she wanted to say something.

"Go ahead and say it," he said.

"I don't have the right to an opinion," she replied, "but I have a question. Are you financially able to take a break for a while?" She held his gaze with her sapphire eyes, as if piercing his soul. "I know the death has been hard on everyone, and it might be best to slow down for a bit. Too much change all at once can be difficult, especially for Ivy, who just lost her mother. Can you imagine what it would be like for her to have to adjust her whole life suddenly?"

"I hate to sound childish and immature, but coming here is asking me to give up everything. I have a job and a life too."

She took several deep breaths before responding. "Raising a child is a full-time job. If you think your mother could provide for Ivy, it might be the best thing."

"Is that why you don't have any children? You weren't up for the commitment?"

The light in her eyes seemed to dim. "No, not at all. I always wanted kids, but never found a guy I could stay with long enough to have them."

He laughed. "You sound like my sister. My mother had everything planned for Chloe, from the wedding to the husband to the house, but Chloe wanted none of it."

"I can't blame her. Who wants someone to choose for them?" She sighed. "Then again, arranged marriages have a higher success rate than unions of love. Maybe it's because they go in knowing what's expected. It's like a marriage of convenience. What about you? Have you ever thought of marriage?"

Frowning, he said, "Marriage looks inconvenient from my end. I'm not a good catch. On paper, I'm everyone's dream. I've got a job, money, and assets, but I'm gone all the time."

"Marriage isn't for everyone," she said.

"For someone who owns a wedding planning business, I'd say that shouldn't be your motto."

"But it's true."

"Are you marriage-averse? Seems to me that's counterproductive to what you're trying to sell."

"Oh no, I think marriage is wonderful, and the best part about it is the wedding." She smiled. "It brings everyone together to celebrate love and life. It highlights the importance of family and togetherness. Which brings me back to my original question: considering your financial situation, maybe you owe it to yourself and Ivy to give Willow Bay a shot. She needs someone who understands her situation and can provide her with a home and family; if you do that, that would be a genuine gift of love for her. Still, it's ultimately up to you. Have you asked her what she wants?"

Chloe wanted Ivy to have choices, but did she mean this? Ivy was five. Was she even capable of making tough choices? He smiled at that thought. "You're right. I should ask her."

"It's a start."

"Thank you for being here, Charlotte," he said as he finished his coffee and rose to put his mug in the sink. "I am grateful for you."

"I'll see you soon," she said.

He walked past the table of treasures and glanced down at the red glass. "If you want to pretend it's a ruby, I'll swear to it."

"It's a ruby," she yelled from the kitchen.

It might be just red glass, but Charlotte was a diamond in a world of cubic zirconia.

When he walked across the yard and into the house, he didn't feel any less burdened, but he felt better. Sometimes, all a person needed was a smile and someone to listen.

Rachel was in the kitchen pouring bowls of cereal. Ivy was on the floor, tying her shoes. At least today, she was in matching clothes. She hopped to her feet. "This was Mommy's favorite dress."

He took in the red dress with the embroidered ladybugs on the pockets. "I love it, and I'm sure your mom would love it too." He appreciated she was wearing color. Chloe loved color, and he didn't want to dim her memory by wearing something as dull and drab as black to her funeral. "I have a red tie. Should I wear it?"

Ivy nodded. "Does it have ladybugs?"

"No. I'm sorry."

"That's okay. We can get you one sometime, and then we can match."

He couldn't imagine what shopping for ties with Ivy would look like. He suspected all his conservative ties would find their way to the back of the closet, and character ties would take a starring role in his attire. "Hey Ivy, would you rather stay with Uncle Bast or Mee-maw?"

She hugged his leg. "I already told you. It's just you and me, kid."

CHAPTER NINE

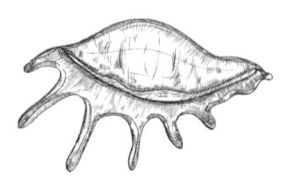

Her coffee rendezvous with Bastien had cut into her day, so she quickly rushed into her room and changed from her casual garb into clothing appropriate for work and a funeral. Charlotte refused to wear black to a memorial service. While it was the end of Chloe's life, it was also a celebration of the life she lived, and life was lived in color. She decided on a deep purple dress—dark enough not to draw attention from the town's gossipmongers but light enough to bring her joy.

As she drove to Because You Said Yes, thoughts of her never-ending bills swirled in her head. Maybe she had chosen the wrong profession. Not everyone got married, but eventually, everyone died. Funerals required the same planning—location (often the church, but sometimes a restaurant or banquet hall), flowers, music, food—lots of food! When she arrived at her shop, Charlotte sat in her car and looked at the window. She felt a twinge of pride as she took in the sight. But that pride was soon replaced by a wave of dread. She needed a paying customer and needed one now.

She couldn't bank on these mommas dreaming about a wedding in the distant future.

She sighed heavily and stepped out of her car to unlock the door so she could prepare for the day. When she stepped inside, her heels didn't hit the polished concrete, but two inches of water and it was raining inside her store with several spots dripping water like a sieve.

"What the hell?" She removed her shoes and ran barefoot to the backroom to see where the water had come from, but outside of the water, everything was in order in her store. A gushing sound came from the common wall she shared with the candle store, and when she glanced at the floor, she could see a steady stream of water rushing in. One touch of the drywall and she knew it was a disaster. Her finger without much pressure poked straight through as if she was a hot knife and the wall butter.

She sprinted to the shop next door and banged on the locked door, but no one answered. Next, she bolted to Cricket's to get Mamie's number. She didn't know the woman who'd come into town this year well, but Cricket knew everyone, and Charlotte was sure she'd have her phone number.

When she burst through the door, Cricket stared at her. "Where's the fire?"

Charlotte threw up her hands. "I don't know, but I've got enough water running in my store to put it out. Mamie's store is flooding, and it's ruining everything. Do you have her number?"

Cricket raced to her office in the back of the diner and came out with a number on a sticky note. "Is everything okay in your store?"

Charlotte hadn't surveyed the damage, but she feared the worst. She quickly dialed Mamie's number, and after several rings, it went to voicemail. With a heavy heart, Charlotte hung up and called the fire department, who assured her they'd dispatch someone as soon as possible.

When Charlotte returned, she observed the damage with a heavy heart. Not only had every piece of furniture been drenched, but all of her lovely display cases and linens were also ruined. Everything was sopping wet, and she feared it would eventually peel or crumble. Her beautiful shop would look like a wedding dollar store if she didn't find a way to save it.

She trudged out of the store and phoned Mamie again. Unfortunately, the voicemail answered again, and Charlotte hung up in frustration. She headed over to Mamie's shop and knocked on the door.

She arrived to find the water was still leaking from beneath the door. She could hear loud noises coming from within, and soon a woman cracked the door. It was Mamie. Her eyes widened in surprise as she took in Charlotte's frantic state. "I'm so sorry."

"Everything is ruined." Charlotte wanted to cry but couldn't allow herself to do that, or she'd bawl all day. Besides, she was expected at Chloe's memorial and couldn't show up looking like a wreck. She had to be strong for the family. Charlotte filled Mamie in on what had transpired while they stood in front of the gushing doorway. "I'm so sorry," Mamie apologized. "An old pipe burst and ran all night long. My insurance will cover everything."

"Is the water turned off?" Charlotte asked.

"Yes, the water and the electricity are both off."

This shot a current of worry through Charlotte, and she rushed back to her store, through the floodwaters, to the breaker box, despite knowing it wasn't safe. It wasn't smart to leave the power on, either.

She walked back, feeling low. Even if insurance paid for damages, it would take too long for her to get back up and running with clients. She was doomed.

Moments later, the fire department arrived. There wasn't much for them to do but suggest a restoration company, whom she called right away. Being a small town, they came thirty minutes later and assessed the damage.

Unfortunately, nothing could be saved of what had been destroyed in the flood. Everything was ruined. Almost all of her furniture needed replacing, not just drying out; linens were stained beyond repair; display cases were warped; and the entire store smelled musty from the water that had seeped into every crevice. It was a total loss.

And when the man handed her the estimate to do the clean-up and repair what they could, she almost wished the breaker box had electrocuted her. She didn't have the money to do the repairs, but knew if she didn't hire them, in days, her store would be covered in mold, and every dream she had would be dead.

"When can you start?" She didn't know where she'd get the money, but she said a silent prayer to the universe to send her a miracle.

She handed over the keys, grabbed her bag and shoes, and pulled the wedding dress off the mannequin. She hoped that Lola's Dry Cleaners could salvage it, and she'd at least have one piece of her original dream left.

She glanced at her phone and knew she had enough time to drop the dress off, go home, touch up her makeup, and head to the funeral.

FRAZZLED DIDN'T COME CLOSE to how she felt, but at least she didn't look like she'd been dragged through the mud, rinsed off, and then used as a doormat! When she arrived at the church, she parked under a big tree and watched as people filed in the door. She was sure that only a handful had met Chloe, but hundreds showed. Southerners were like that. It was good manners and a great time to try a new recipe.

Inside, people were chatting in hushed tones with somber expressions. A few folks stopped to hug Charlotte as if she were the one grieving. It made her feel bad that she hadn't taken the time to get to know her neighbor. She scanned the crowd, looking for Bastien, Ivy, and Rachel. She found Ivy and Rachel sitting in the front pew. Ivy hugged her teddy bear and held the tenderly adorned envelope in her hand. Rachel looked bored and as if she would rather be anywhere else in the world. Where was Bastien?

She moved down the aisle and approached Ivy.

"Charlotte!" Ivy called out, her voice ringing through the quiet room.

"Hello, Ivy, how are you, honey?" She ruffled Ivy's bangs and then carefully finger-combed them back into place. "I was looking for your Uncle Bast. Do you know where I can find him?"

"He went out that door with Mee-maw." She pointed to a door at the side of the building.

"Thank you."

"Are you coming back?"

"Yes, I'll be back soon." She walked to the door and exited to find herself in a courtyard full of memorial plaques. The morning sun cast a beautiful golden hue on them. She spotted Bastien down one path and headed towards the old graveyard where his dark hair peeked above the tall stone wall. As she neared, she heard a conversation between him and a woman. She stopped on the other side of the wall, not wanting to interrupt. She figured when a lull in their conversation occurred, she'd show herself.

"I've filed a motion to gain custody of Ivy," the woman said.

"Mom, you know full well that's not what Chloe wanted."

"She had cancer. She obviously wasn't in a good place to make sound decisions." A low, unladylike growl filled the air. "What was she thinking? You're not fit to raise a little girl. Hell, you've been known to date them."

"That's absurd and untrue."

"The last woman you dated was thirty, and you were forty-five."

"I'd hardly call her a child."

"You're a bachelor, and a small girl shouldn't be exposed to your single, work-hard, play-hard lifestyle. A couple with a solid, longstanding marriage must raise her. No court is going to award custody to a playboy."

Charlotte knew she should skedaddle before things got too heated, but she couldn't bring her feet to move.

A long, slow whistle floated above the old stone wall. "And you and dad are the model for a solid marriage?"

His mother scoffed. "We've been married for over fifty years."

"Happily?"

She spat out a response. "No marriage is always happy."

"You don't even live together. Dad lives in London with Eve, and what's the name of the pool boy of the month?"

A sharp slapping sound came from the other side and sent Charlotte running toward the door. She hurriedly took the seat next to Ivy and would stay until Bastien and his mother arrived, and then she'd find a seat farther back in the pews.

A few moments later, the door opened, and a dour-looking Bastien entered, followed by his smiling mother.

Ivy dropped her bear and grasped Charlotte's hand. "Don't leave."

She was torn because she had no place sitting in the front pew with the family, but she didn't have the heart to abandon Ivy.

"Who are you?" Mee-maw asked.

Charlotte opened her mouth to speak, but Bastien answered for her.

"This is my good friend, Charlotte." He took the seat beside her and kissed her cheek. "Thank you for coming."

Sandwiched between Ivy and Bastien, she felt both out of place and exactly where she needed to be.

The service was short and beautiful, and as they passed the casket, Ivy put the letter she'd lovingly crafted inside. They made their way down to the church's kitchen, where enough food to feed an army was laid out.

Stuffed to the gills with cornbread casserole and Mabel Huntley's ham biscuits, she made her way to the door. She'd leave the family to their grief. She had some mourning to do herself. She was drowning in expenses and now Because You Said Yes was drowning in water. How would she get out of this pickle she found herself in?

CHAPTER TEN

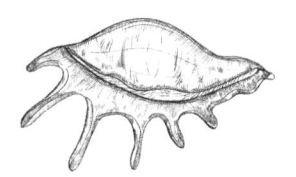

Bastien had never liked funerals or cemeteries, but he'd visited both today. Despite the occasion's somberness, some relief accompanied him as he stepped away from the graveyard and into the open air. Next to him, Ivy and Rachel were both lost in a world of their own thoughts, but even in the silence, he could feel the weight of their shared grief.

Stepping out into the street, the sun was high in the sky, a reminder of life's unyielding and ever-hopeful cycle. Bastien realized that despite the day's sadness, they still had to go on living. They had to move forward. The living, even when left behind, had a responsibility to live fully. That was the rule of life.

Without saying a word, he turned to Ivy and Rachel. "You must be hungry." Even as he spoke, he felt his stomach grumble as if it knew what he was thinking. He recalled the dozens of casseroles that virtual strangers sent to their door. He didn't have the energy to do something as simple as reheating any of them.

"Cricket's," Little Ivy said matter-of-factly.

Still sullen but unable to resist the lure of food, Rachel shrugged and said, "I could eat."

Bastien couldn't help but smile. It was a moment of normalcy that felt like a bit of freedom. He nodded in agreement and started his car, driving off into the glow of the afternoon sun. The streets were busy, which was a welcome respite from the stillness of the graveyard.

The inviting red neon "Open" sign shone from Cricket's diner and beckoned them inside. The restaurant was quiet, likely because of the time of day; it was already past lunch but too early for dinner.

They took the empty booth under a poster of a rooster that read, *I don't give a cluck*. Bastien didn't give one about much, either. That impromptu meeting with his mother shook him. Chloe said she'd fight for custody, but he didn't think she'd do it at the funeral.

Cricket arrived wearing her red high-tops and a smile. "What can I get you?"

Ivy said, "I'll have the regular." It made him wonder how many times she'd been to the diner.

Cricket looked at Rachel. "BLT and leave off the bacon?"

Rachel shook her head. "Might as well indulge. I ate pepperoni last night."

Cricket laughed. "And it didn't kill you?"

She must have seen the sadness etched across their faces because she suddenly looked apologetic. "Sorry," she said quietly, before writing their order on her notepad and grabbing a menu for Bastien.

He scanned the menu, unsure what he wanted. He felt like he could eat anything right now to shut out all the emotions bubbling up inside him: confusion over the custody matter, grief over losing Chloe, and regret for not being here more. Finally settling on a double cheeseburger and fries, he handed Cricket back the menu before turning his attention to his niece and the nanny.

"Ivy, how are you doing?" he asked, his face softening into a kind smile.

"I'm good," she said.

He nodded, then shifted his attention to Rachel. "What about you?"

Rachel's mouth tightened into a thin line. "I didn't sign up to work 24 hours a day. It's against the rules, and I'm not getting paid enough for that."

He ran a hand through his hair. "I understand. I'll make sure you get compensated for the extra effort. I know it was a tough time, and I'm thankful you went the extra mile."

Rachel smiled, her face softening as she looked away from him. "Thank you," she said.

Rachel was burdened by expectations no nineteen-year-old should have to bear. She didn't have the life experience of an adult yet, but he had asked her to take care of Ivy. It was like asking a child to care for another child. He'd have to get more help quickly.

"How many hours per week do you work?"

"I'm contracted for 45 hours a week. I can't exceed that amount."

He thought about his job, which required frequent absences, and how he'd need multiple nannies to make it work. "What would happen if I had to leave town?"

She shrugged. "I've only worked for Miss Chloe, so I couldn't say for sure, but rules are rules."

He was not a fan of rules, but the world was full of them.

Cricket reentered the room, balancing a stack of plates

on one arm and chocolate milk, diet soda, and orange juice on the other.

"Here you go, sweets. Let me know if you need anything else." She grinned and winked. "Like another cup of my special brew?"

His stomach turned. "I'll stick with the Diet Coke for now."

"Let me know if you change your mind."

He wouldn't and picked up the soda and took a deep drink, relishing the feeling of the cool liquid bubbling down his throat.

Ivy dug into her chocolate chip pancakes while Rachel deconstructed her BLT, moving the bacon to the side.

"I thought you wanted the bacon."

She sighed. "I did, but now my stomach aches."

"Should we stop at the five and dime and get you something?"

"No." She sighed heavily. "I have to tell you something."

A knot formed in his belly as he anticipated what she might say, and he was suddenly overcome with dread.

Rachel took a deep breath before she spoke. "I've been thinking about going back to California to go to college. It's the best thing for me right now," she said.

Bastien frowned and looked down at the table. "Can you give me a week or ten days? I need to fly back to New York to settle a few things."

"You want me to work 24 hours a day for seven to ten days?" She looked up at the ceiling and then back at him. "It's going to cost you."

"You said you couldn't work over 45 hours in a week. I'll try to find you help."

She shrugged. "I need dorm room money, so I'll do it. I

won't tell if you don't. But I expect overtime for anything over 45, and I can't drive."

His jaw dropped open. "What do you mean you can't drive?" He cut his burger in half and took a bite.

"I can drive, but I misplaced my driver's license, and haven't taken the time to replace it."

He swallowed and wiped the ketchup that oozed out the side of his mouth. "Okay, no driving."

"You'll have to find a way for Ivy to get to school while you're gone."

With a slight tilt of his head, he asked, "How was she getting to school before?"

Rachel hung her head. "Chloe had to drive her."

His heart sank. His sister barely had the energy to breathe at the end, yet she had summoned enough strength to get up and drive Ivy to and from school each day.

He didn't know how he was going to pull it all together, but he'd figure it out.

The door opened, and Charlotte and several women walked in. They all crowded around her, patting Charlotte's back, and telling her they would help with whatever they could. He wondered what had happened.

She drifted past him, looking slightly dazed, to a nearby table, pulling her lips into a smile that Bastien could see immediately didn't seem to reach her usually bright eyes.

He watched as one woman grabbed her arm and pulled her in for a hug before taking a seat. Charlotte slowly sank into the chair, looking forlorn, her eyes glossy and her brow furrowed. Was she grieving because of the funeral, or had something else happened?

He slowly stood and made his way over to them, unsure of what he would say when he got there. When he reached their table, he could only manage a soft, "Are you okay?"

"Heavens, yes." She seemed to rise in her seat, and the taller she got, the brighter her smile became. "These are my friends." She pointed to a beautiful woman with honey-colored hair. "This is Emmaline." She pointed to the brunette in the group. "You probably know Marybeth. She's the minister's wife." She nodded toward a stout woman with graying hair. "That's Tilly. She's the chef at The Kessler."

Cricket arrived and said, "You won't be able to remember them, but they call themselves the Fireflies." She chuckled. "They like to think it's because they bring light in the dark, but it's because they're as pesky as any insect."

He stepped back and half-bowed. "Nice to meet you, ladies. I'm Bastien Richmond, and for now, I'm living next door to Charlotte."

"Who is single," Marybeth added.

Bastien smiled. "So, I've heard."

Charlotte rolled her eyes and gave her friends a pointed look. "I don't have time for romance," she said firmly. "I already have enough problems in my life; I don't need to add any more by getting involved with someone."

"Anything I can help with?" Bastien asked.

"You know how to fix flood damage?"

He shook his head. "I'm not what you'd call the handy type."

Emmaline waved him off. "Then what good are you? A man who can't fix something is about as useful as tits on a boar."

He chuckled. "I'll take my leave." He was about to turn when he realized he still needed help. "Do any of you have kids in the school? I have to leave town for a bit, but I need to find a ride for Ivy to get to school."

Charlotte raised her hand. "I can take her."

Marybeth cleared her throat. "I volunteer at the library in the afternoon, so I can bring her home."

"I'm happy to compensate you for time and gas," Bastien said.

Tilly snickered. "You're not used to small towns, are you? We take care of our own."

"No, I'm a city boy." He was beginning to understand the concept of Southern hospitality and was thankful that his sister had chosen a place that was so welcoming.

"Not anymore. Now you're part of our family," Tilly said.

Until that moment, he had one foot in and one out of Willow Bay. In New York, he didn't have a support system. He lived in a luxury condo with one bedroom. It technically had three, but one he'd turned into an office and one into a gym.

"I appreciate all your help. I feel like a fish out of water."

Emmaline smiled. "You better get back to the lake, or Cricket will dip you in cornmeal, and you'll be the next blue plate special."

"I'll take that as my cue," he said.

"Not at all," Charlotte said. "Y'all are welcome to join us."

Emmaline shook her head. "Another time, maybe. We're interrogating her for information, and she's using you as a shield."

"That's something I've never been used for. Other things, even money, yes ... Shield? No."

"You can't say that anymore. It's another thing to add to your resume."

"You think there's any money in being a shield? It looks like I'm taking a sabbatical from my job for a bit."

Charlotte's face lit up, her mouth stretching into a wide smile. "So, you're staying?"

"For Ivy," he said.

Charlotte's expression grew even lighter, and she clapped her hands excitedly. "That makes me happier than a tick on a fat dog!"

He tried to picture that. "That's pretty happy." He turned and walked back to the table, thinking about Southern customs like funeral casseroles and southernisms. He was born in Atlanta and, by all rights, should be a Southern gentleman, but he had been raised in boarding schools in the northeast, so he wasn't completely familiar with the customs of the South—or their charming phrases.

CHAPTER ELEVEN

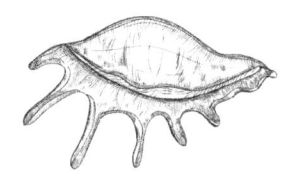

After an hour with her friends, Charlotte, usually full of energy, felt like she'd run through a gauntlet. When her friends offered their help, she forced a smile, thanked them, and said she had it all under control. That was the furthest thing from the truth, but she was determined to handle it on her own. She had relied on others her whole life and longed for the ability to rely on herself. The setback for the shop wasn't the end of her dream, but an obstacle she had to hurdle. She needed money but had no intention of asking for help from her friends.

As she walked out of the diner, a sense of dread washed over her. She turned toward the shop to find her entire inventory and furniture on the sidewalk in front of the store. In piles strewn across the cement were waterlogged linens, sample invitations, and floral arrangements. Her stomach lurched as she took in the damage. The storefront looked worse than it had when she took it over. It had once been a rock shop that sold everything from geodes to meteor chips, and now it looked like it had been hit by the latter.

A man from the restoration company approached,

carrying a shelf with swollen wooden feet and peeling paint.

She rushed over to speak to him. "How long do you think it will be before I'm back in business?"

He looked at the mound and whistled. "We'll be done in a week or so. The bigger question will be how soon you can replace what was ruined." He glanced at the damage. "How good is your insurance?"

She pointed to the candle shop next door. "It's her insurance that will pay."

"Good luck with that." He moved back inside, leaving her with more questions than answers.

As a business owner, she was required to have multiple types of insurance, like a general liability policy to protect against personal injury and property damage. She had professional insurance, which Charlotte liked to think of as whoops insurance in case she messed something up or forgot the cake topper and got sued. She had to have insurance for her storefront as well and purchased the cheapest policy she could find. Charlotte knew cheap wouldn't equate to good but needed to call her insurance to report the loss, regardless. That was a job for tomorrow because all she wanted right now was a bottle of wine and a seat by the water.

HER TOES MOVED through the sand as she walked to the water's edge with a bottle of cabernet, a glass, and a blanket. Charlotte faced the water, closed her eyes, and inhaled, letting the salty air fill her lungs and wash away the stress of the day. She set up camp on the shore and cracked open her liquid relaxation. As she poured herself a glass, she watched the afternoon fog roll off the gulf, enveloping her in its embrace.

Charlotte waded into the shallow surf and let the sand squish beneath her toes. She took a sip of wine from her glass, the warmth sliding soothingly down her throat. Gradually, the knots in her chest loosened, and tears pooled in her eyes. The thoughts of the flood that had delayed her dream, the funeral she had attended for her neighbor, and how her friends had looked at her with pity, came cascading forward in emotions too strong to bear.

She loved building that business and was looking forward to running it. It was heartbreaking to see it damaged by something out of her control. But as she gazed at the water and sipped her wine, she watched people stroll along the beach hand in hand. Families and kids ran around playing and enjoying the moment. It was an uplifting sight that reminded Charlotte that even when life threw curveballs, there was still beauty and love to be found amidst it all.

"Aren't you cold?" a deep voice said from behind her.

She spun on her heel and immediately saw Bastien. He had traded his navy-blue suit for a pair of faded jeans and a black T-shirt. All she could focus on was the taut muscles that lay beneath. The transformation was astounding, and Charlotte's breath caught in her throat.

"Hey, it's you." Surprise mixed with strange excitement coursed through Charlotte's veins as Bastien stepped closer, leaving only a few inches between their bodies. She met his gaze, his eyes dark and intense. The warmth radiating from him swirled around her, causing her mouth to dry and her cheeks to heat.

"It is," he replied. His lips were drawn into a slight smile that showcased his pearly white teeth and set off a wave of sparks deep within Charlotte's chest. "I didn't mean to startle you. Am I intruding?" he asked.

"No, it's just—I had a long day, and seeing you here is..." She stumbled over her words, not wanting to say something ridiculous or something she would regret.

"Surprising?" he asked.

Charlotte's heart skipped a beat. Why was she feeling this way? Out of all the myriad emotions flooding her senses, why did attraction have to be the one that surged forward? After all, there was nothing remotely arousing about her predicament.

"Yes, a pleasant surprise," she admitted before looking towards the horizon and changing the subject. "I thought you'd be with Ivy."

He kicked at the sand with well-worn boat shoes. "It was a rough day, and she fell asleep." He gestured to the blanket and the bottle of wine, half-submerged in the sand, a few feet away.

Charlotte smiled. "I understand how that can be." She paused to think, then asked, "Do you want to sit down? I don't mind the company." It was funny how she couldn't wait to escape her friends but was happy to spend time with Bastien.

"Will you share your wine?"

"I only have a single glass."

Bastien chuckled. "You can share that too. I left my cooties in New York."

"I'm happy to share." She moved from the water to the blanket and patted the spot beside her. He kicked off his shoes and took a seat.

They sat close enough that their arms were almost touching. Charlotte's heart raced, but she refused to let this man make her feel flustered, like a schoolgirl with a crush.

Bastien took the glass and filled it with wine before holding it out to Charlotte. She took it from his hands, and their fingers brushed against each other, sending a frisson of awareness through her body. The last time she'd felt that much charge from a touch was when she climbed out of her bedroom window to sneak a kiss with Brandon Bellows. She'd been sixteen.

Ignoring the stirring sensation, she raised the glass towards Bastien in a toast. "To new beginnings," she said.

"Yes, to better things in the future," he replied before taking the glass and a sip for himself. "Are you sure taking Ivy to school isn't a burden? I know you're busy with the business and stuff."

Charlotte felt her chest tighten as she thought of her shop. Bastien must have sensed her distress because he put an arm around her shoulder and pulled her close. Charlotte looked into his eyes and saw compassion there.

"As it turns out, I'm going to have some time on my hands." Charlotte opened up, telling Bastien what happened with her business today—the tragedy, and everything she'd lost due to it—but she didn't let him know how dire her financial situation was.

"I'm sorry about your shop," he said, squeezing her shoulder gently.

She leaned into him, feeling his embrace, and allowing it to soothe the sadness that had taken root in her heart. She laid her head on his shoulder. "I'm sorry about your sister." Charlotte knew this man had seen much pain in his life—she'd met his mother.

Bastien sighed and nodded but didn't take away his arm from around her shoulders. Instead, he kept it there for a few moments before releasing it and turning to face her.

He cupped her cheek and leaned in. She was sure he

would kiss her. She didn't know how she felt about that. Part of her wasn't ready for anything else, but part of her was. She leaned in, but instead of his lips touching hers, he said, "You'll rebound from this setback—I know you will." He finished by giving her one last hug before standing up and sliding on his shoes. "I need to get my travel plans settled. If I can head out tomorrow, I can be back by early next week."

"I'm here if the girls need me." She'd never been a mother, but she'd been around her share of children and teens and figured their issues were generally solved with a hug, a meal, or a laugh.

"It makes me feel better that you're here. I appreciate you."

"Do you have your phone?"

He pulled it out of his pocket and handed it to her. She tapped in her phone number. "In case you need me for something important, like, I don't know, a pizza run!"

He immediately sent her a message. When she pulled her phone from her pocket, she found his text.

> Thanks for being a good human.

As he walked away, she turned towards the shoreline as the sun slowly began its descent.

CHAPTER TWELVE

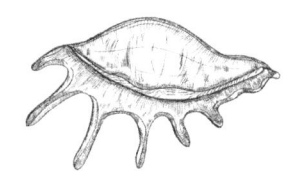

Bastien was lucky enough to find a commercial flight out the following day to New York. He usually used private jet consolidator services for flights, but his assistant could find nothing available from Galveston on such short notice. That was fine. He'd use the extra time at the airport and on the flight to get himself organized. He had a lot to take care of and little time to do it. He knew he needed to go through Chloe's end-of-life folder, which contained her will, but it was too soon, and he felt too raw to deal with it. He settled back into his first-class seat and closed his eyes, thinking about the days that had passed and the ones to come. He had managed so far to sustain the veneer of everything, including his emotions, being under control. But for how long?

His thoughts raced. It was hard enough to say goodbye to Ivy, who made him promise he'd come back to Willow Bay. Was she worried he would abandon her? While he didn't intend to make the sleepy town his permanent home, he knew he could give it a few months until Ivy had settled into the idea that he was her sole guardian, and they would need to make some choices. She needed time to adjust to the situation.

He chuckled to himself. Who was he kidding? It was he who needed to adjust to the situation. For all intents and purposes, he was now Ivy's dad. No matter what his intellectually dishonest and manipulative mother thought. Granted, he wasn't a father or a husband, but he was a damn good uncle and brother—even if he had never settled down. One thing was sure, he would never lead a life of deceit and philandering like his parents. He knew the difference between right and wrong. And he knew we are known by the commitments we keep, not by the ones we make. That alone would make him a better example for Ivy. And it was the key to his success in business as well.

It's true, he had thrown himself into his work, avoiding romantic entanglement that he might end up pretending never happened, much like his father had done in the past. But Bastien reminded himself it wasn't like he didn't forge meaningful connections in life. He could be a father. He was not the lone wolf playboy his family had made him out to be. He mentored and helped build the careers of many talented young men and women who worked for him. There was great satisfaction in watching them grow and develop, and he had earned their trust and respect. He supported up-and-coming artists, sponsored scholarships, and funded many educational and sports programs for kids. People obviously thought he was a good guy or there would not have been so many invitations for him to be a godfather. Right? Wasn't all that enough? He could be there for Ivy. He knew it.

As he flew from Galveston to New York, in between racing thoughts of his qualifications to be a parent, his beautiful sister, and the life she had left behind, he traded emails with his secretary and planned to turn over his clients temporarily to someone he trusted. He'd never been happier to own Richmond Wealth Management. While he was a hands-on CEO, he'd hired some of the best people—competent and loyal enough to steer the ship while the captain was away.

The plane ride to New York had been a jumbled blur, and as the plane descended into LaGuardia, he sent a text to Charlotte to check how things were going.

> Hello Charlotte, I'm checking in to ensure that Ivy and Rachel are doing alright and nothing else has gone wrong.

Charlotte. He had hardly given her a thought during his machinations throughout the flight. Was it because thinking of her conjured her expressive face, her thoughtful gaze and how her presence somehow made it seem like everything was going to be alright? She had made such an impact on Ivy, who barely wanted to leave her side. And Bastien admitted Charlotte had affected him too, but he wasn't sure if that was a good or bad thing. He hardly had room to make sense of and accept the loss of his sister. He was not ready to consider, consciously or otherwise, that Charlotte could be anything more than someone to help in the way she was already. Besides, he needed her help desperately, and he wasn't about to mess that up, for Ivy's sake. Anyway, she had made it abundantly clear she wanted nothing more, either. He needed to respect that, too. Bastien put any thought of something more with Charlotte out of his head. He had other things to do than allow himself to fantasize about relationships that, based on his life experience, were only fantasy at best.

He wasn't one to borrow trouble, but trouble seemed

hot on his heels the last few days. In his world, trouble looked like his seventy-year-old mom. She had a face frozen by Botox but a piercing glare that could slice through him like a hot knife through butter. She had the patience of a hungry dog and the attention span of a hummingbird's wing flitting from one place to the next.

How was she supposed to raise a five-year-old? Oh, that's right. She'd hire in help until Ivy got old enough to send away. That's what she'd done with them. In hindsight, it was probably the best thing that happened to him and Chloe. Their parents didn't raise them. They were nurtured by well-paid teachers who cared more about them than Annette and Sebastien Richmond did. It wasn't like that for all the kids. Many had warm, loving families waiting for them at home. For most, boarding school was a way to enhance a child's learning experience and social environment, but for the Richmonds, it was a way to have children but not have to deal with them. His mother took "children are to be seen and not heard" to a whole new level. She took out the seen part and largely banished them from the time they were born.

The plane landed, and he quickly exited. His phone sounded with a text alert as he rushed toward the terminal.

> Hey, Ivy got off to school just fine. She asked me to walk her inside, which I did. I also arranged for school lunch for the week since Rachel forgot to pack her one. All's well here.

He hadn't thought about school lunch. He'd left several hundred dollars on the table if they wanted to order pizza or needed groceries. He didn't know what emergencies the girls could encounter but wanted them to have resources if something came up.

> Once again, I'm grateful to you. You always seem to be there when we need you.

He found his driver waiting by baggage claim, and since he had no luggage, he could go straight to the car. Traffic was heavy, and it took nearly an hour to get to his Tribeca loft. That was one of the many arguments he had with his mother. She thought he should live on the upper east side, where many of her socialite friends were, but he loved his view and appreciated all the fine dining available within a few-block radius. They would have been neighbors if the young John Kennedy had been alive. That certainly would have made his mother happy.

He paid the driver and walked into his building. Tony, the doorman, greeted him with a smile.

"Welcome home, Mr. Richmond."

"Hi, Tony."

The rotund man with a balding head fumbled to open the desk drawer and retrieve a large manila envelope. "This came for you today." He passed it across the desk. One look at the return address of Bexley and Brown Attorneys at Law and he knew exactly who it was from. His mother wasted no time putting her lawyers to work. She was probably on the phone the second he pulled away from the curb at the airport. Or, knowing her, she had it in the works before she left Atlanta.

"Thanks, Tony." He pulled out his wallet and tipped the man before he walked to the elevator. The ride to the tenth-floor penthouse was short—there were no lofts in skyscrapers in Tribeca. Bastien's *Architectural Digest*-worthy apartment was perfectly appointed, but he knew his heart and his life were not—a fact driven home like a lightning strike by the envelope from his mother's lawyers still in his hand.

He unlocked the door and stepped into the dimly lit foyer. Introspection was not Bastien's strong suit, but he was seeing that his sister's dying wish might be as much for his benefit as Ivy's. He thought he'd find comfort in the familiarity of his place, but all he came home to was the smile of the doorman, albeit sincere, and what felt like cavernous space with a sweeping view. At least it wasn't the soul-less shrine to capitalism his mother would have wished on him, but the chic loft he had fought to win in a battle of bids suddenly didn't feel like home either. He'd never had time to make it one. Homes develop a vibe and a soul from the laughter, love, hopes, and dreams shared with the people who inhabit or visit them. Bastien's endless client meetings, the creative cocktail parties, his fleeting relationships, and the weekly visits from the housekeeper had not filled his apartment with more than the odd fading fragrance, dropped drink, or superficial memory of a good time. *Had it taken his sister's death to realize this would-be pleasure palace was not a home?* Bastien wondered.

At the same time, thoughts of funerals, wills, and work obligations swung back into his consciousness, leading to a feeling of exhaustion that threatened to overwhelm him. He knew he needed to focus on what responsibilities lie ahead to take care of Ivy, so he poured himself a glass of wine and opened the lightning bolt.

Laid out in front of him was his mother's attempt to bury Chloe's wishes. But he'd made a promise, and he intended to keep it. Wasn't it enough they had just buried her?

He dialed his mother and listened to the phone ring

three times. His mother believed that answering on the first or second ring gave the impression of desperation, like you had nothing better to do in your life than wait on their call. Letting it go to the fourth ring was pure disrespect for the caller. The third ring, in her mind, was the perfect timing.

"Hello, Bastien. How can I help you?"

"Are you seriously suing me for custody of Ivy? That's not what Chloe wanted."

Annette sighed heavily. "Yes, I've filed for custody of Ivy. You know it's best for Ivy, and if Chloe had been in her right mind, it's what she would have wanted," she said in a sharp tone.

He knew his mother didn't like to be challenged, but he also knew he'd never betray Chloe's deathbed wishes for her daughter. She had entrusted him to take care of her daughter, and he would not let her, or Ivy, down.

He spoke firmly but calmly, "How do you know what she would have wanted? You never asked."

"We weren't talking."

He sighed. "She talked to me and told me under no circumstances did she want you taking Ivy."

"She would have never said that."

He laughed. "Not to you, because she knew how you'd respond, and she didn't have the energy to fight you. She made me promise, and I'll fight you every step of the way."

"All I want is what's best for my granddaughter, and I can't believe Chloe imagined it would be you."

He tried to remain calm as he responded, "And what do you believe is wrong with me?"

Annette replied with a hint of anger, "I don't think you are capable of taking care of a child or that you'd even want to. You're always so busy. Too busy with work, too busy with women, too busy thinking only of yourself. What kind of life would Ivy have with you? You're constantly traveling and working."

Bastien released an exasperated exhale. "I'm making the necessary adjustments."

"If Chloe chose you, it's because she thought it would be easier on me."

Bastien nearly dropped the phone. It was like his mother to make everything about her and twist and turn the narrative to fit her needs. Chloe didn't spare her final thoughts for a mother who treated her like a designer accessory. She thought only of her daughter and what was best for Ivy. Bastien knew that.

"No, she wanted Ivy to have the choices she never got until she reached adulthood, like what to wear and who her friends were. And she wanted her to grow up free of superficial judgment."

His mother made a dismissive sound. "Choices come with maturity. She wasn't ready to make them until she reached adulthood. And look at how Ivy dressed the day you picked me up. She's not capable of making those choices, either. She looked like you'd picked her up from a homeless shelter. And that you let her out of the house wearing that makes me think you're not ready to make choices for her."

"Maybe not," Bastien conceded, "but at least I know being a parent comes down to more than how to dress a child. I'm going to make sure Ivy has all the opportunities and chances that Chloe didn't get as well as all the love she deserves. That's why I'm here."

"Who will talk to her about girl things like boys and menstrual cycles? She needs a mother figure. You can't even keep a girlfriend. Who is going to be there for Ivy? Who can understand what it means to be a girl, a woman? You're a wheeler and dealer. She's a child who lost her mother. No court is going to give you custody of a vulnerable child when there is a stable and reliable set of grandparents who are clearly superior guardians. That's just a fact."

He was now in way over his head, but he wasn't a quitter, and he certainly would not allow his mother to steal the dignity of his niece the way she had stolen and squandered both his and his sister's. Without thinking of the consequences, he blurted out, "Well, it's a good thing that I'm getting married then." He didn't know why he told a lie. It just bolted from his mouth before he could engage his mind.

Bastien's words hung in the air, shocking his mother into silence. Hell, they shocked him too.

After a long pause, she said, "You're getting married soon?"

"Yes. I'm sure that my fiancée would be happy to help Ivy with any girl issues. And any judge will see that a loving and devoted couple will be best suited to provide Ivy with the home she deserves." He was doubling down. Loving and devoted couple? He didn't even believe that existed, but he was going to make it look real, at least for Ivy's sake.

"Why haven't I heard of this before today?"

"Because we don't talk. It seems to be a universal theme with your children."

"Don't be cruel. When will I meet this mystery woman?"

He knew if he didn't get off the phone now, his mother would grill him for more information—information he didn't have.

"We'll see you in court."

He ended the call and gulped his wine. The reality of the conversation was setting in. And the reality of what he'd be up against in court. How was he supposed to find a wife before their first court appointment? He looked at the documents in front of him and saw the date. He had exactly thirty days.

The reality of the situation and the emotion of the confrontation with his mother forced the sting of loss to pierce his being, opening the floodgates of Bastien's grief for the first time. His head fell into his hands as he heaved tears like gutters unable to contain the cloudburst of a storm. His body quivered as his heartache and all the losses that came before, including the death of his little sister, fell from his eyes, and he cried out in pain as never before. Time seemed to stand still. The catharsis slowly ebbed, bringing with it the seeping realization that Bastien was alone in a place that didn't even feel like home.

CHAPTER THIRTEEN

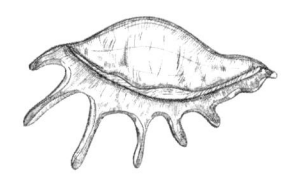

Charlotte waited by her car for Ivy to come out dressed and ready for school. When she didn't show up, Charlotte got nervous, walked next door, and knocked. No one answered, so she pounded on the door a little harder. She waited a few seconds and tried the door, but it was locked. Panic swept over Charlotte like an icy wave from the shore.

A thousand scenarios went through her head from kidnapping to carbon monoxide poisoning. She was dialing 911 when the door handle rattled, and Rachel appeared in the doorway looking frayed and disheveled.

She stood motionless and blank. "What time is it?"

"It's after eight. Where's Ivy?"

Rachel stared at her like she was speaking a foreign language. "She must be asleep."

Charlotte marched into the house and past Rachel. "Where's her room?"

Rachel scrubbed her face with her palms and pushed her tangled hair out of her eyes. "It's the second door on the right. We had a late night."

"Late night? She's five. How late could her night have been?"

Rachel knotted her hands together. "I was filling out college applications, and I lost track of time. We got to sleep around two or so."

"Two o'clock in the morning?" Charlotte moved down the hallway toward Ivy's room. "I thought you were a trained nanny?"

"Well, I am, but I made a mistake."

"I'd say." Charlotte got to the closed door and eased it open. She peered into the room decorated perfectly for a five-year-old with unicorns and princesses, and swirls of vibrant colors adorning the walls on one side, and posters of pioneering women from Amelia Earhart to Maya Angelou on the other. Charlotte thought the eccentric mix of fantasy and ingenuity was a fitting combination for Ivy, who had such a natural curiosity and zeal for learning. Ivy lay slumbering peacefully in the middle of her bed surrounded by stuffed animals. Her hair swirled around her head as if she'd just stepped off a wild ride on one of the unicorns.

The sight brought a smile to Charlotte, and then she remembered why she was there. It was now half past eight and Ivy was late for school. She turned to Rachel and whispered, "I can't believe you allowed her to stay up so late on a school night. That was totally irresponsible!"

Rachel hung her head as she followed Charlotte into the room. "I know. I'm so sorry. There's been so much going on the past few months. I just got lost in what I was doing. Just please don't tell Bastien about this. Ivy was happy reading. Time just got away."

Charlotte glanced over at Rachel before turning back towards Ivy, who was slowly waking up from the ruckus she'd created earlier. She stroked Ivy's hair soothingly with one hand. "Ivy, honey, it's time to get up. We are already late for school."

Ivy peeled her eyes open, one at a time. "Charlotte, you're here!" She sat up and wrapped her arms around Charlotte's waist. It was as if Charlotte had been part of Ivy's dream.

"Good morning, ladybug." She didn't know why she called her that, but maybe it was because she always seemed to wear them. If her memory served correct, Bast called her a bug. She was certainly as cute as one. The ladybug variety, not a wolf spider, or her least favorite insect, a cricket. She'd never tell Cricket that, but she had a good reason for not liking them. When she was a child, she got swarmed by them and several got stuck in her hair. It was a disaster from the beginning. First the crickets, and then she ran directly into a spider web, which caused her to panic, so she bolted in the other direction and stepped into a gopher hole and fell, breaking her arm. While she was getting her cast—a pretty pink one—her mom was combing out grasshopper carcasses from her hair. In the end, she went to Dolly's Do's, where Charlotte was subjected to her one and only pixie cut.

"Can I stay home from school? I'm tired," Ivy pleaded as she flopped back onto her pillow and pulled the covers up to her chin.

Charlotte smiled, picturing the moments when she was young and wanted to skip school. "No, honey. You need to go, but why don't I take you out for breakfast before that? Is that a happy plan?" Ivy was behind schedule already, and it was critical to get her to school with food in her tummy and ready for the day and Rachel didn't look up to the task. "I'll give the school a call and let them know we're running late, but that you'll be there."

Ivy nodded before throwing back the covers and climbing out of bed. Calling her ladybug was perfect as she wore pajamas covered in them and butterflies.

"Will you help me dress?"

Charlotte nodded. "Yes. I'd love that." She opened Ivy's closet and found it filled with fun, colorful clothing that made her smile. After laying out an outfit for Ivy, Charlotte helped her get dressed.

Once her teeth were brushed and her long locks put in pigtails, Ivy and Charlotte headed off to the diner for breakfast. Rachel stayed behind to pull herself together.

In Cricket's Diner, they sat below the sign that said, *It Ain't Cocky If You Can Show What You Crow*. Charlotte looked around the restaurant. The next poster was a rooster and said, *Nice Cock*. Next to it was another that said, *Rise and Shine Mother Cluckers*. She hadn't taken in the "artwork" but now that she had, she found most of the posters wildly inappropriate for a family restaurant, but funny.

"What's it going to be?" Cricket said as she approached, pulling out her order pad and pen. She leaned over and pulled on one of Ivy's pigtails. "You're becoming a frequent diner here. Soon enough, you'll be in the kitchen cooking your own breakfast."

Ivy beamed at the thought. "Can I?"

"Not today." Charlotte didn't need to look at the menu. She'd been coming there since she was a kid. "I'll have my regular." Her regular was bacon and eggs with crispy hash browns and sourdough toast.

Cricket lowered her pad and smiled at Ivy. "And what will it be for you?"

Ivy sat up as tall as she could. Her chin barely cleared the tabletop. "I'll have the regular too."

Cricket started writing and stopped. "Would that be your regular or Charlotte's?"

Ivy cocked her head. Kids were so expressive. "Is hers better than mine?"

Cricket laughed. "Nope, no chocolate or whipped cream."

Ivy's nose crinkled. "I'll stick to mine."

Cricket reached over and gently tapped the end of her nose with the pen.

"She looks good with you. Is there something you want to tell me?"

"I'm the morning driver."

Cricket looked at her watch. It was the size of a coffee saucer. "I'd say you're late."

"There was a failure in the system."

"Charlotte to the rescue?"

"Something like that."

"Like I said," she glanced between Charlotte and Ivy. "This whole domestic thing looks good on you."

"It's temporary. Her uncle will be back soon."

Cricket leaned in. "He'd look good on you, too." She pivoted and walked off before Charlotte could respond, but that did not stop her cheeks from flushing at the thought.

Seconds later, her phone rang, and Bastien's name scrolled across her screen. Another flush.

"Hello," she answered.

He cleared his throat. "Is everything okay? The school called and said Ivy didn't come today."

She got so distracted dressing Ivy and doing her hair that she'd forgotten to call them. "I'm so sorry. Rachel and Ivy slept late. I figured Ivy needed to eat before school and seeing the shape Rachel was in, I didn't want to leave that up to her, so I brought her to Cricket's Diner. I intended to call the school, but I forgot. I'm so sorry."

He let out a deep exhale. "I'm relieved. I thought maybe my mother had absconded with her."

"Would she do that?"

"I wouldn't put it past her these days." A phone rang in the background. "I have to go, but when I get back, can we talk? I have something I need help with."

"Yes, without a doubt."

He hung up, and she thought about what he might need. A new nanny, for sure. Realtor, local secretary, tutor? It hardly mattered because it looked like she'd have plenty of time on her hands and was more than willing to help. Just that morning, Charlotte had spoken to the insurance company, and she was certain that she had made serious errors, most notably hiring the restoration company before the adjuster arrived at the location. Everyone knew she shot first and aimed later, and this was no different. Her knee-jerk reaction was to hire someone right away. With any luck, the restoration team had taken photos of the store before they began the work, in addition to Charlotte's photos of the space after being finished.

Cricket set down two drinks—a coffee and a hot chocolate—alongside the breakfasts they had ordered. When Charlotte asked for the bill, Cricket shook her head.

"Not today. It's part of the Willow Bay flood relief fund."

"Cricket, I'm not a charity case."

Cricket shrugged. "I know. So ... let's pretend this is like one of those casseroles we deliver. Let's face it, your shop bit the dust. Seems appropriate."

She had no words except, "Thank you."

"I'm not charging for the meal, but don't skimp on the

tip. The waitstaff here is top-notch." Cricket laughed all the way to the kitchen.

Ivy ate her pancakes and drank her hot chocolate with enthusiasm, while Charlotte only ate a few bites of hers. She was too stressed to take much pleasure in the meal. Although Cricket's kind gesture of providing breakfast had brightened her day.

Finally, it was time to go. Charlotte left a generous tip and said goodbye to Cricket before heading out with Ivy. They got into the car and drove a few blocks until they reached the school.

"Don't forget to go to the library after school and Marybeth will bring you home. You'll eat school lunch all week." She pulled through the drop off lane and one volunteer opened the back door for Ivy, and she climbed out. She took off running toward the door but stopped and turned around and blew Charlotte a kiss.

Her heart felt like it would explode with happiness. She blew Ivy a kiss back and watched her disappear into the crowd before turning around and heading back home.

Now she would focus on what she was going to do about the store. She was determined to get it restored and running again as soon as possible. She had no choice.

As her car came to a stop in the driveway, Charlotte noticed Rachel was sitting on the front porch swing while a suitcase was propped on the first step. Her initial feeling of warmth from saying goodbye to Ivy was replaced by an icy sense of dread.

She climbed out of the car and made her way to the porch. "Hey Rachel, what's up?" She stared down at the suitcase.

Rachel stopped swinging and rose to her feet. "I can't do it anymore."

Charlotte stood still, bracing herself for what she knew was coming. Rachel bent over and gripped the handle of the suitcase before stepping closer, so that only a whisper of salty air passed between them. "What can't you do?" Charlotte asked, leaning against the banister for support.

"I messed up last night, but honestly, my heart isn't in any of this. It was a summer gig and summer ended weeks ago. I didn't sign up to be an end-of-life nurse or a full-time mother. It's just too much. If I leave now, I can still enroll in a few classes, but if I don't, I'll have to wait until next semester, and I don't want to wait that long."

"Did you tell Bastien you're leaving?" By the looks of it, Rachel wasn't staying another second, and Bastien wasn't around to take over.

By the fall of her head, she knew Rachel hadn't before she shook her head. "I don't know what to say."

"Exactly what you told me."

"I know, but he'll try to talk me into staying."

Charlotte took several breaths. "What about Ivy?"

Rachel clasped her suitcase to her chest and shut her eyes tight. "Can you watch her until he returns?" Tears slid down her face. "It's too much for me to handle. I watched her mom die and teach her little girl to accept it, move on, and keep her memory alive with joy and a love of life. Damn, I barely knew her and I'm not moving on, let alone feeling joy. I don't feel like I can live up to Ivy. She's five and handling life better than me. I don't want any of this. I'm 19 years old, not old like you." Charlotte bristled a little at the thought of being called old, but she got the point. "People are expecting way too much from me. You all live in some kind of bubble where everyone pitches in and looks after each other. It's great until it gets real, and I end up taking the place of a dead mother to an active little girl twenty-four hours a day. I have to go."

Charlotte, while taken a little aback, was aware of how much despair people could feel, and of all the demands Rachel had been subjected to. Rachel's ability to articulate that so clearly in the moment, and that any self-awareness lurked beneath her generally disinterested demeanor, surprised her though. Rachel was right. Even temporarily, it was too much for her alone.

"We'll call Bastien together," she suggested softly.

Rachel seemed to fold in on herself as she nodded.

Charlotte walked inside and went right to the kitchen, where she turned on the kettle and pulled out some tea bags and honey. Tea and sympathy, she thought. It couldn't hurt. No one had been listening to Rachel much. Maybe an attentive ear could bring her back, at least until Bastien could get back to Willow Bay.

Once she got their tea ready, she sat across from Rachel at the small table and dialed Bastien. He picked up after a couple of rings.

"Good morning, Charlotte, is everything okay?" he asked.

Charlotte took a deep breath before explaining what was going on.

"Umm, there's a hiccup in the plan. Rachel has decided she cannot continue her duties."

In the background, there were soft murmuring voices, and then there was silence. "Sorry, I was in a meeting. Can you repeat that?"

"Rachel has quit. She is no longer up to the task, understandably so. She's been through a lot for her nineteen years, and she wants to dash back to college."

"I had a feeling she might. How much notice is she

giving me?" Charlotte covered the phone. "Rachel, when is your flight?"

Rachel extended her arm, showing her outstretched palm with five fingers splayed wide.

"Five hours."

He released a sharp breath. "What? How am I supposed to find someone to replace her in five hours?" His voice cracked and splintered as it climbed in volume.

Charlotte took a breath. "I can take care of Ivy until you return." She had a lot on her plate already, but she had taken to Ivy and Ivy to her. She looked forward to more time together.

"I can't ask you to do that."

"You didn't, I offered. We'll be fine." She may never be a mother, but that didn't stop her from wanting to nurture someone. "It'll be fun for both of us."

"Are you sure?"

"Absolutely. Don't worry about a thing."

"I'll see if I can speed up my transition."

"Take your time. We'll be right here."

After they hung up, Rachel sighed and looked down at her teacup. "I'm sorry."

"It's okay," Charlotte replied, taking a sip of her tea. "Do what's right for you. I understand. And I'm sorry your needs got pushed so far to the back and no one acknowledged all that was on your plate. It will be fine, Rachel. Thank you for everything you have done. You can feel proud of the help you provided to Chloe and Ivy."

Rachel finished her tea and stood up. "Thanks for hearing me out and for being so understanding," she said, squeezing Charlotte in a tight embrace.

"I get it—go live your dreams. You deserve them as much as anyone else. Never let anyone tell you otherwise."

She stepped away and asked, "Do you need a ride somewhere?"

Rachel shook her head. "No, I arranged for a car to pick me up at the diner. I think I'll go there now on foot to clear my head. Please tell Ivy goodbye for me. I wouldn't know how to tell her myself."

Charlotte walked Rachel out of the house and followed her with her eyes until she was just a tiny figure silhouetted against the horizon.

CHAPTER FOURTEEN

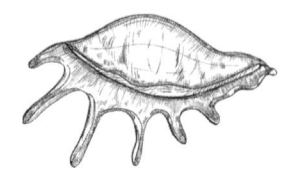

Bastien felt cursed and blessed at the same time. He was in hyper-focused work mode. The grief that had gripped him arriving back in New York had strangely fortified him and strengthened his resolve to get things in order so he could be there for Ivy. He wasn't alone. He had a kid to take care of, to raise, to guide, to nurture into as stellar a woman as his sister had been. Still, he had been counting on Rachel to help in the transition and thought to himself, *Kids these days have no work ethic*. He had a mind to phone the company Rachel worked for and tell them how disappointed he was that she gave him five hours' notice, but it made no difference since Rachel wouldn't be returning to the nanny service, and in truth she had fulfilled her contract for the summer and then some. Besides, he wasn't the client, his sister was, and she was no longer there, so Rachel owed him nothing.

Bastien was grateful for Charlotte, who had stepped in to save the day. She had been a source of support since he met her, and her willingness to help with things had been a godsend. He returned to his meeting and was interrupted again when an "urgent" call from his mother came in.

He exited the meeting room once again, hoping she'd changed her mind about fighting for custody of Ivy.

"Hello, Mother. What is so urgent? Have you changed your mind about turning Ivy's life upside down and dishonoring the wishes of your only daughter?"

"Bastien. Enough. I've called the house several times today, and no one is answering. I want to make sure my granddaughter is being cared for since you are not there."

His mom had an uncanny ability to recognize when something wasn't right, even at a great distance. He wondered if that was motherly instinct when she wasn't busy eating her young. Or just her ability to smell chum in the water. Whatever it was, she was somehow in tune and ready to swoop, as usual.

"Ivy is where she is supposed to be, at school."

"But the babysitter isn't answering, either."

"That's correct. Her contract is complete, and she's being replaced."

"Who's watching my granddaughter?"

"Ivy is in good hands." He reassured himself as much as his mother, but he didn't have that much knowledge about Charlotte or anyone else in town. He had to rely on his sister's judgment. After all, she moved to Willow Bay for a reason other than the house on the beach—though the cynic within him challenged the trusting assumption.

"Is she with strangers? They didn't know anyone there. They weren't there long enough to have friends." He could almost picture his mother's Louboutins pacing inside her newly renovated mansion, etching her anxiety into the hardwood floors. "This is why you're not a good fit. You left a grieving five-year-old with a virtual stranger when she could have been with her mee-maw."

"She's not with a stranger, but there's no bigger stranger to Ivy than you," he replied. Touching the depths of his despair had also given Bastien more resolve to keep his commitment to Chloe and Ivy, even if it meant constant fighting with his mother. "How many times have you seen her in the last year, two years, three years?" He knew she hadn't seen Ivy in person for ages. The only contact she had with her was by video call, and that was infrequent, at best.

"It's not because I didn't try." Her voice carried a note of resignation, or maybe even regret.

He had to believe his mother's heart was in the right place. She would not willfully cause emotional or other harm to Ivy. "Mom, you and Chloe had different opinions on how to raise a child."

"And you don't know anything about children. What makes you a better choice than me?"

He had to concede he knew little about children and was still convincing himself he was the best choice to be Ivy's sole guardian. "I was Chloe's choice. There is nothing more to say."

There were several seconds that passed where everything was silent. "I'm going back to Willow Bay and getting my granddaughter. She shouldn't be left with strangers."

He sighed heavily. In order to get his mom to stay where she was, he had to make her feel as if there was no cause for concern. "Mom," he said, "I've been going to Willow Bay for a while now, and my fiancée is there. Ivy is in good hands." Lying was not a comfortable place for Bastien, but damage control, in this case, required stretching the truth. Who was he kidding? This wasn't stretching. Right now, unicorns were more real than a fiancée waiting for him in Willow Bay.

"Did I meet her at the funeral?"

"I'm sure you did," came the reply.

"What was her name again?"

He wanted to end the conversation, if only to avoid his mother flying out to Texas. "You're only asking for a name so you can research and stalk her online, aren't you?"

"Is there something wrong with that?"

"Not at all."

"So, tell me a name, then."

"Why can't our family just be like everyone else and live in peace?"

She sighed. "Because I have difficult children."

"They say your children are a reflection of yourself." He hoped not, but if he put the blame on his mother, she'd retreat.

"I have tickets to the Philharmonic and can't miss the concert, but I'll be there in two weeks, and I want to meet this fiancée and see Ivy."

He ended the call and leaned back against the wall, rubbing his tired eyes. He could feel a slight panic rising in his chest. Thirty days to find a way out of his dilemma had just been compressed to fourteen. Now he had only two weeks to find a woman willing to pose credibly as his fiancée. He was stuck between a rock and a hard place and time was fleeting as usual.

He informed his team that the meeting was over and that he'd keep them posted while he was gone. He gave a senior executive authority, had his secretary book a flight, and left. His business could continue to run in his absence. He had to get out of there. By being away from Ivy and Willow Bay, he was causing more damage than good.

He rushed back to his loft and packed a bag full of casual clothes and one suit. On his way out, he told Tony to hold down the fort. He honestly couldn't say when he'd be back. His flight would leave in a few hours, and he had just enough time to get back to the airport.

He sent a message to Charlotte.

> I'm on my way.

She replied promptly.

> There was no hurry. I was overjoyed to look after her. Ivy is such a delight.

> I know, but I need you to help me with something else.

He wondered what Charlotte would say when he asked her to find him a wife.

> What do you need?

This wasn't a conversation that should be handled over text.

> Did you mean it when you said you could get anything a person wanted?

> Within reason

He knew his request was unreasonable, but he'd have to ask, anyway.

> Let's talk later when I get back. It will be late. Where can I find you and Ivy?

> Consistency is important for her, so I'll be at your sister's house. That way, she can sleep in her own bed and be surrounded by familiar things.

> I'll see you soon.

He tucked the thought about consistency away to be used in the future if needed. It could be a persuasive argument to convince the court to let him keep Ivy instead of giving his mother custody, or worse yet, forcing them into some kind of shared custody arrangement. However, he knew that staying in Willow Bay would be necessary for this plan to work. He wasn't one to preach one thing and practice another, and he knew Charlotte was right.

WHEN HE REACHED THE HOUSE, Charlotte was in the living room reading a book. He dropped his bag and sat on the sofa across from her. "Thank you for everything." The hospital bed was gone, and the space was free of clutter—all Charlotte's work.

"I hope you don't mind that I had it removed. It was a heavy weight in the room, and I find it's always better to remember someone when they were at their best."

"I agree. Thank you. How's Ivy doing?"

Charlotte smiled. "She was excited to come home and find me here. We played in the sand and built a castle big enough for a princess. She had a little homework—"

"She's only five. How can they have homework?"

"I'm proud to tell you she has no problem with her alphabet. Did you know she can read?"

Bastien's chest puffed up with pride. "She reads at a third-grade level."

"She's incredible," Charlotte said.

He stood up from the couch. "She is. Mind if I go check on her?"

"Not at all. Would you like a glass of wine?" she asked.

"That would be wonderful," Bastien said.

He strolled down the hallway to the second door on the right, comforted to find Ivy fast asleep. Her face appeared tranquil as she lay in the soft caress of the pink nightlight. He paused on the edge of her bed and gave her forehead a gentle stroke before standing. As he walked away, he whispered, "It's just you and me, kid."

He joined Charlotte in the living room. He needed to ask her for a favor, and it would not be easy. He sat down and said, "I need you to find me a wife."

CHAPTER FIFTEEN

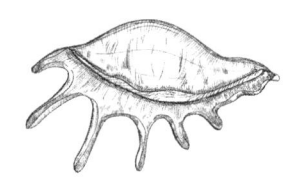

Charlotte nearly spit out her wine and asked, "Did you just say you need me to get you a life—or a wife? That's a rapid progression from a guy who felt it necessary to tell me within nanoseconds of meeting you that you had no interest in relationships or marriage." She stood, looking incredulous, realizing now the remark had stung, even if she wasn't interested either. "You understand I'm a wedding planner, not a human trafficker, right?"

Bastien realized his request had come off a bit abrupt. "I'm sorry. That's not what I meant. I'm not interested in sex."

"Oh, that will make some woman happy! A lifetime with a husband who doesn't want to touch her," Charlotte quipped back. "Geez, Bastien, what's going on?"

Bastien furrowed his brow. "My mother has filed for full legal custody of Ivy."

Charlotte sank to the sofa and rested her hand gently on Bastien's shoulder. "Oh, my gosh! I'm so sorry. Can she do that?"

"She can and will, whether or not it's best for Ivy."

Nobody else would have understood what he meant, but she had witnessed his mother in action. "Is this related to your conversation with your mother at the cemetery?" She felt guilty for eavesdropping, but it's hard to walk away from something like that without paying it some attention. She knew next to nothing about the man and little girl who had waltzed into her life, and it was impossible to turn away from the shock of his own mother betraying him and her dead daughter at her funeral. She'd never even imagined such a thing. She had to hear how it played out. Besides, she had quickly become attached to Ivy and wanted to help her and Bastien.

"How do you know about that?"

"I went looking for you at the funeral and overheard."

He reached for the back of the chair and gently pulled it toward him. His body sunk into the seat as though gut-punched, but not yet defeated. "Then you heard she's dead serious about fighting me for custody."

Charlotte's mind reeled at the thought. She couldn't fathom that a mother—any mother—would be so cold, especially now, when so much had been lost. Her voice barely above a whisper, she asked, "She would do that?"

"The papers were waiting when I got to New York."

Her brow furrowed. She leaned forward and pressed her fingertips together as if forming a bridge. "And you think getting a wife will stop her?" Her voice rose in disbelief as she tried to comprehend his logic. "Wouldn't lawyers of your own be a better weapon for the fight than a fake bride? It's like bringing a cake knife to a gang war."

Bastien smiled at the visual of a cake knife offered by a wedding planner. "Answering my mother's opening salvo with my team of lawyers would be throwing down the gauntlet and putting Ivy smack in the middle of a long, dirty court battle. It increases the risk my mother could get temporary custody, and Ivy could be eight or nine by the time it all got resolved. We'd make all the lawyers incredibly rich at the expense of Ivy's emotional and physical well-being." He leaned forward in the chair. "I wouldn't do that to Ivy except as the last resort. The best weapon is to take the wind out of my mother's sails by proving to her Ivy is better off with me."

Charlotte had also overheard Annette's accusation that Bastien was a playboy, but while deeply interested in his side of that story as a true Southerner, she didn't dare bring it up. She was relieved that Bastien did.

"My mother is convinced I'm a workaholic playboy incapable of caring for a child."

"Are you? A workaholic playboy, I mean. I know you're not incapable. I've seen you with Ivy."

"Workaholic maybe before. Playboy, never. I built a large and successful company with the most wonderful and loyal employees and clients who value our ethics above all. It's not the *Wolves of Wall Street*, for heaven's sake. But I worry my mother's self-serving accusations could be an easy sell to a judge and social workers with the papers and TV full of stories of soul-crushing, morally bankrupt financial Svengalis."

Charlotte felt herself growing closer and closer to Bastien. At the same time, he explained that he had not had time for long-term romantic relationships and that his most important friendships were with people who worked for him, whom he had mentored and developed. Bastien assured her there were no stories of orgies or other debauchery. Still, the truth of being holed up in conference rooms for weeks at a time, itineraries like flying from New York to Shanghai to Zurich to Dallas in three days, and the 90-hour work weeks might be just as damning. He would be described as someone who puts work above all else and isn't available. Charlotte could see Bastien was someone who put others first and took his responsibilities seriously. She could see how a court would not give him credit for developing a team of people who could operate largely without him, as they were doing now. It would be much easier for people to stereotype him as another greedy fund manager who probably did something wrong to achieve success, not the hardworking investor in people and ideas he was.

While she never knew Chloe, she understood why the dying mother would choose Bastien to raise her spirited and darling little girl. He would be her first choice, too.

"Bastien, this is awful, but is a wife the answer?"

"I don't want a wife, but it would seem I need one. And I've already told my mother I'm getting married."

He pointed to an armchair opposite him, and she settled into it, folding her hands in her lap, ready to be educated on how a man who was adamant against getting married was now trying to find a wife.

He grabbed the bottle of red wine Charlotte had put on the counter earlier, pulled the cork with a loud pop, and filled his glass until it was almost overflowing. He offered her a top-off, but she shook her head and covered her glass with her palm. "I'm good. Thank you."

"I wish I were." He drank deeply and sighed. "I don't know what happened, but I was talking with my mother, and she pointed out all the reasons I'm unfit to care for Ivy." He ran his hand through his hair and sighed. "She might be right."

Charlotte reached out and placed her warm, soft hand atop his. "I know this is a lot. But I'm sure it's just like any other new parent experience. Just with an extra wrinkle."

He laughed, the sound thin and raggedy. "Most parents don't give birth alone to a forty-pound bundle of energy and sass that can talk. A five-year-old, no less."

She tried to think of the positives. A wry smile crept across her face. "At least you don't have to worry about midnight feedings and diaper changes."

"I suppose that's true. Anyway, my mother pointed out everything that made me unsuitable, and then she started talking about how Ivy would need advice about boyfriends and women's things."

Charlotte rolled her eyes. "Ivy is five. She won't have a boyfriend for quite some time, and while women's things will come faster than you'd like, you still have a lot of time. You don't need a wife. You need a few books."

"I panicked and told her I was engaged and that my fiancée was more than willing to step in and help."

That sounded like something Charlotte would do; she was often known to act quickly without considering the consequences, so it was easy to envision and empathize with that situation. Her sympathy for Bastien was growing deeper, along with her affection for him. He was less and less a stranger, and she couldn't help but like him more and more.

"And now you need a wife," she said.

"Well, a fiancée. It would be better if I didn't have to go through with the marriage, but I will if I need to. I'll do whatever it takes to keep Ivy with me."

"Again, why not hire a bunch of lawyers?" She snickered. "Probably cheaper than a wife. Obviously, this isn't a long-term deal, and divorce is expensive and messy." She understood why an army of lawyers wasn't the best first move but thought lightening the mood with a joke might take the edge off a little.

He leaned back in the antique wooden chair, its frame creaking in protest against his athletic body. He clasped his hands behind his head and fixed her with a stare. "It's not a real marriage," he said, "just a marriage of convenience." His muscular arms and strong chest created a pleasant view that did not escape Charlotte's attention, along with his fixed gaze. She redirected her focus to the conversation.

"That sounds pretty inconvenient," she said as she pondered what it meant to be in a sham marriage. Was it only for formality and on paper, living separately, or was it a marriage in every sense with a fast expiration date and a hefty payout? Would he be willing to pose naked for prospective wives? Should she try him first so she could offer an actual endorsement? *Focus, Charlotte!* she admonished herself silently. No more wine for tonight.

"It's not ideal, but it's for Ivy, and I'd do anything for her."

She suddenly loved that about him. From what she could see, Bastien would make a great husband. "Why are you so against marriage?"

"I've never seen a happy one." A growl rasped from his throat. "Can you believe she's using her marriage to my father—a man who didn't even show up to his daughter's funeral—as a selling point to take Ivy?"

Charlotte hadn't even thought about Bastien and Chloe's father. She supposed it was good he wasn't hovering to take Ivy away, too. "How long have they been married?" Charlotte asked.

"Fifty years," Bastien replied grimly.

"That's commendable." Fifty years of marriage was something to be admired. While she couldn't understand why Bastien's mom was so adamant about taking Ivy, she could appreciate her desire to keep their family together.

"Look, my mom isn't a horrible person; truth be told, she wasn't even a horrible mother, or at least that wasn't her intention. She was the product of upper-class self-absorption, and so-called values that forced her to marry at a young age after a ski trip to St. Moritz led to a romance which led to a missed period and then me and a shotgun wedding."

"But they stayed married for fifty years, so it must have been okay."

"I'm sure she thought she could love my father. It worked out on paper, but not in real life."

Charlotte thought about what marriage had looked like for Bastien's mom. Fifty years ago, women didn't have children out of wedlock—not nice, refined women. "She's a product of the times."

"Maybe. All I have to say is she figured it out mighty fast and forged a future for herself. She hired nannies and followed my father around the world to keep their fragile alliance together."

"And you felt abandoned?"

"I was abandoned, but maybe she and I aren't all that different. Maybe she did what she did for what she considered the greater good. I'll do the same for Ivy."

Charlotte had seen a lot in her fifty years. She'd seen families like the Browns destroy their children's lives in order to continue the family fortune. She'd seen relationships ruined for property, money, and appearances.

"Did she ever try to get close to you and your sister?"

"Early on, she was on the high-speed train of endless social engagements, charity work, travel, and high society fundraising events to save everything from whales to lost masterpieces. Holidays, semi-annual family vacations, and school visits afforded the semblance of being engaged in our lives, but we didn't see it that way. It always seemed like Chloe and I only had each other."

Charlotte thought about living in a home where she didn't feel loved and couldn't imagine it. She'd been the apple of her parents' eyes.

"One thing is certain. You both learned how to be independent." It was the single fault she could place on her parents. As an only child, they'd doted on her and ensured she always had enough, but she rarely had to do anything for herself. She's never learned to be independent. Even after their deaths, they'd set her up for success, and she'd messed that all up.

"We learned our place early on, and it wasn't sitting on mommy's lap."

"But they're still married. That says something."

"I suppose it does," he said. "It speaks to their stubbornness to give up anything, including a failed marriage. My parents haven't seen each other in years. Theirs is a different kind of fake marriage. I'm fairly certain my father believes it's cheaper to keep her. Maybe my mom is in the camp that it's better to stay with the devil you know."

She'd never understand that. Her parents were married for over forty years before her father passed. She couldn't remember when they were apart except to go to work and run to the store.

"Marriage is a sacred act." She rubbed her temples as if to ward away a headache. "I'm sorry, but I can't find you a temporary wife."

"But you said you can get me anything. Charlotte, you are well-connected, and people like, trust, and respect you. You're creative and energetic. I have nowhere else to turn."

"Bastien, I'm a wedding planner, not a matchmaker. Brides to Go doesn't exist."

He set his jaw in stern determination. "I don't see why not. After all, Nannies R Us is where Chloe found Rachel."

"Well, we know she'd leave you at the altar. You get what you pay for."

"I'm willing to pay. How does $75,000 for trying sound?"

Her jaw dropped. "You're offering me $75,000 to find you a wife?"

"I'm offering that if you try, but I'll pay you double if you succeed. I need a wife, and I need one now." He grimaced as if the words burned his lips.

"Please don't say no. Take the night and consider it. Surely, someone will exchange their time for money, especially to help a young girl who has just lost her mother."

"How much time do you have before the court hearing?"

"It's thirty days to the court appearance, but my mother is coming here in two weeks to check on Ivy, and she wants to meet my fiancée, of course. I can't prevent her from coming. Depriving a young girl who had just lost her mother from her grandmother would look terrible to a judge. And I don't want to do that to Ivy either. She needs all the love there is."

Charlotte couldn't understand why someone would marry for money rather than love. That was a big reason she started her wedding-planning business: to give couples the perfect day. She knew that most marriages didn't outlast their honeymoons, but she wanted to believe that marriage had to have more purpose than money.

"I want to help you and Ivy, but I just can't," she said with finality, shaking her head and pushing away from the table. "I won't knowingly facilitate something so wrong."

He exhaled slowly, then nodded. "Fine," he said, though

something in his voice told her he wasn't giving up just yet. He reached across the table and placed his hand over hers, surprising her with the warmth of his touch. "But will you at least think about it? I'd do anything for Ivy, and I'm sure you understand that."

Charlotte pulled her hand away slowly and stood up. She knew what it meant to protect those we love, and she admired Bastien's dedication to his sister. But this wasn't something she could get behind—not even if it meant helping his brilliant niece.

"I'll think about it," she said before quickly turning around and walking away from him, not wanting him to see how conflicted she felt about his offer. "Are you good for the night?"

He followed her into the living room and then to the door, where he opened it. "Yes, we'll be fine."

She picked up her bag by the door and walked out. As soon as she was out of sight, Charlotte wondered what kind of person would agree to a marriage like this. Was someone out there desperate enough—or perhaps even crazy enough—to go through with such a plan? Despite her misgivings, Charlotte felt obligated to at least look into things for Bastien's sake, if for nothing else. After all, if he succeeded in keeping Ivy safe from his mother's grasp, that would be worth any cost or risk, wouldn't it?

She entered her home and went straight to the kitchen, turning on the kettle and preparing a cup of tea. When she opened the drawer to find her honey dipper, she was greeted by a stack of bills that screamed, "pay me." She pulled them out and tossed them on the table. They slid across, and one fell to the floor. When she picked it up, she saw the mortgage company's logo. She was already forty-five days behind on the loan she took against the house. How long would they give her before they took her house?

She poured her tea and sat there staring at the money she owed. A glance around her kitchen made her see the blinking light of her home phone. She rose and pressed in the code to retrieve the message.

"Hello, this is Maxine Felder from Prime Mutual, and we'd be happy to send an adjuster out. What about a week from Wednesday?" Charlotte didn't listen for the number. All she heard was a week from Wednesday. She knew her shop would eventually get put back together, but that didn't help her today.

When she went into business, she had a plan. She knew she was supposed to have at least a year's worth of working capital, but thought she'd be okay with six months. She didn't expect things to cost so much to begin with. Then again, her sense of luxury hadn't conformed to a budget.

The message stopped abruptly with a beep, only to be replaced by a soft voice on a second message. It was Lola, whom she had asked to repair her beloved dress. But when the word unsalvageable was uttered, Charlotte felt a wave of misery wash over her. As much as she wanted to believe there was still hope, the tears that streamed down her cheeks told her otherwise. She wanted to scream and cry out in frustration, yet all she could do was sob into her hands.

She knew she had no other option. She needed the money, and Bastien was the only one offering any. With a heavy heart, she reached for her phone, her hand trembling as she composed the text. None of this felt right, but there was no other way.

Gripping her phone, she punched out a message.

> Alright, I'll do it.

She placed her phone back on the table and sipped her tea. Not once in her life, when she considered being a wedding planner, did she ever think she'd have to supply the bride. How was she going to pull this off?

CHAPTER SIXTEEN

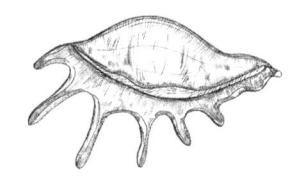

B astien searched the diner for a quiet corner after dropping Ivy at school, but it was even busier than usual. Charlotte insisted on meeting, and breakfast that wasn't Cocoa Puffs sounded good. "Hi there, Bastien," Cricket called as she directed him to a tall booth at the back. "Charlotte told me you were meeting and needed some privacy. I'd say get a room, but we hardly know each other, and Charlotte's not that kind of girl," Cricket teased. Bastien chuckled at the irreverence.

"Can I bring you some of my killer brew?"

"No killer anything today, please. I'd be happy with just a small injury of regular coffee if you don't mind. Bastien remembered his body's involuntary response upon learning the origin of Cricket's "secret brew." That would have been a tough visual to crush, but for Charlotte bursting through the door laden with what looked like sample books, fabric swatches, papers, and a briefcase.

"He's over here, darling," shouted Cricket with a full-arm wave as if guiding a yacht to its berth. "I put you guys in the confessional." So much for privacy, Bastien thought, although while anyone and everyone now knew they were there, it would be difficult for anyone to overhear their conversation. He guessed that was best because he didn't know exactly what she wanted to discuss so urgently.

Charlotte had said she was stopping at Because You Said Yes on the way to salvage what she could of some of her catalogs and stationery before the cleaning crew unceremoniously conveyed them to the dumpsters in front of the store with everything else. The cleaning crew had arrived as if on a mission from God to remove any and every "stain" in their path, no matter how small the transgression. Anyone else would have looked harried and disheveled, but as always, Charlotte appeared as if she had just walked off a page of *Southern Belle*, with her demeanor just as buttoned up. "Hello, Bastien. I'm so sorry I'm late. It's been quite a morning." She let everything in her arms fall to the middle of the table.

"Can I help you with that?" offered Bastien.

"No, thank you. I need just a minute to get organized." Anyone taking in the scene would have guessed he was her next client, he thought. That could be a good thing.

Cricket laid down a menu and a glass of water on the table by the window, not close to, but within view of, "the confessional." "What's your pleasure?" she asked the man sitting there. "You look like a sculpture, honey," Bastien overheard her say. "Those baby blues are the same color as your t-shirt. Pretty as a cloudless sky!"

The stranger smiled. "I'd love a coffee, black, please. That's all."

"Ooh, I've got just the thing for you. I call it my out-of-towner brew. Wanna try some?"

"How can I resist? I couldn't help noticing the mess across the street. Fire?"

"Oh, no. A pipe burst and flooded not only the candle shop, but my friend's new wedding planning business next door," Cricket offered. "It's a shame. She just opened and everything is ruined."

While Charlotte was singularly focused on organizing her haphazard cargo into manageable piles, Bastien's ears perked as he, and anyone within a country mile, heard Cricket talking about Charlotte's store with the man. To Bastien, he looked out of place in the breezy beach town of Willow Bay, but Bastien could recognize a city guy anywhere. They tried hard to look relaxed, but the manicures, designer T-shirts, posh haircuts and a slightly condescending air when confronted with people who had chosen less complicated lives were dead giveaways.

"That is a shame. Is Willow Bay popular for destination weddings?"

"I guess it could be. Is that what brings you here?" Cricket laughed. Bastien wondered if she was trying to figure out whether the guy was eligible for a good time or not. "You know, we haven't had many real 'lookers' in town since summer ended."

"I'm just passing through. Thought a couple of days near the water would be a nice break before my next stop."

"What is it you do?" Cricket asked. Her interrogation skills weren't subtle, but that seemed to be Cricket. Looking at her red high-top sneakers and T-shirt with red sequins that read Eat Me, there was nothing subtle about the diner owner.

On their first encounter, Cricket was not shy about asking for details from anyone, especially someone who could be the object of some shameless, and he assessed harmless, flirtation. Something about her jovial and unassuming manner was disarming, and he imagined it made people reveal their secrets as if speaking to an old friend.

"I'm a loss prevention consultant. I help business owners deal with insurance companies before and after a catastrophic event."

"Oh, my God. I should put you in touch with Charlotte! She's lost everything, and it seems like her insurance company is moving slowly."

"Is Charlotte the wedding planner? I'd be happy to meet her if you think it would be helpful. Her situation doesn't look complicated."

Charlotte turned briefly, hearing her name, but she turned back to Bastien as if he was all that mattered in the moment. Despite the disaster that awaited her at the shop, she seemed singularly focused on him, but he imagined it was the big paycheck he offered that kept her tuned in. When Cricket mentioned the insurance, Charlotte gave Cricket and the stranger a polite look that said, *I see you, and I'll deal with you later, but not right now.*

"Good morning, Charlotte," said Bastien with a smile. "It's nice to see you."

She looked up from her organized piles. "Oh, my gosh, I'm being so rude. Sorry. I just needed to make some room on the table in a way that wouldn't end in a pile on the floor. Did you order already?" She sat back and sighed.

Cricket appeared. "Charlotte, my customer over there is a loss consultant or something like that. He helps businesses with insurance companies," she said excitedly. "He was asking about the bad luck mess across the street and said he would be happy to talk with you. Maybe he can help speed up the insurance payments, since your company is dragging their feet." Charlotte seemed suddenly flustered. Bastien was suspicious of the offer and the stranger's interest but waited for Charlotte's response.

Cricket was visibly disappointed when, instead of jumping at the chance, she barely looked up and murmured, "Oh nice, thanks. Maybe later."

"Hmm. Well, ok then," Cricket said. "If you don't need help to get those blood sucking bastards to pay what they owe you." She pulled her order pad and pen from her pocket. "What can I bring you two?"

They ordered, and Bastien spoke with some embarrassment. "Charlotte, I apologize. I've never asked how you're doing with the disruption of your business, and if there was any way I could help." He noticed her face flush and hoped he had not offended her with the question. She was one of the most capable and self-sufficient women he had ever encountered. How else could he entrust her with helping to unravel his own plight?

"It's all fine. Thank you. I don't need to burden you or anyone with my problems. There's nothing more important to me right now than helping you and Ivy from being dragged through a fire by your mother's lawyers. Let's get started."

Charlotte took out a notebook and was suddenly all business. Bastien was slightly surprised by the "take-charge" manner but knew enough about Southern women to sit back and comply or face the consequences.

She leaned in and whispered despite their cocoon like environment, "I've got some questions about your ideal wife."

"My ideal wife is no wife," Bastien mused.

"That's not funny!" she shot back. "How can I find someone to fulfill my commitment when I've got zero inkling of what you would find attractive in a woman? Don't you think your mother will see through the ruse and use it against you if it's obvious to her and everyone else that the engagement or marriage is a sham? I've got to do better than slap lipstick on a pig and stick it in a wedding dress."

Bastien knew Charlotte was right, but he hardly saw the point in baring his soul when all he needed was someone who was plausible and amenable to their arrangement.

"Bastien, please. I'm not trying to pry or embarrass you, but we have little time and Ivy's happiness and childhood are riding on making this work. The urgency isn't lost on me. I've made a commitment and can move much more quickly if you give me something to work with."

"For starters, she should breathe and be able to stand erect," he joked.

"You're not helping." Charlotte frowned.

"Charlotte, if I knew what I wanted in a woman, I might already have one by now. To avoid a legal battle that might give my mother even temporary custody of Ivy, I'd marry the Statue of Liberty. We don't have to waste time on what would make me happy. This pantomime isn't about me. It's about Ivy and the life she deserves."

Charlotte persisted. "I see your point, but can you give me anything? I know we are not shooting cupid's bow here, but I'd at least like to have a target. Who's your ideal woman?"

The midmorning sun was filling the diner with a golden light that warmed the air and cast a gentle glow on Charlotte's blonde mane and beautiful face. Bastien took in her soft features and saw her passion, earnestness, and her unbridled courage for the first time.

Without saying it, he thought, much to his surprise, my ideal woman could be you.

CHAPTER SEVENTEEN

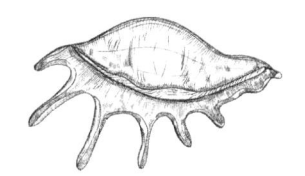

Charlotte's hands trembled as she poured hot water into her mug. She glanced nervously around the kitchen, her gaze settling on the shiny silver tea kettle that was a gift from Emmaline last Christmas. With the flip of a switch, she could have hot water in a minute. Too bad finding Bastien's fake wife couldn't be as easy. She had less than two weeks to complete her task, but it was made harder because the hunt had to remain a secret. Add in that a five-year-old's life was riding on her ability to find a reasonable candidate, and she was as nervous as a cat in a room full of rocking chairs.

As she scoured the eligible women of the town for a suitable companion for Bastien, her list quickly dwindled to three. Margot, a single mother of three whose desperation for cash was written all over her face. Tilly, a friend of Charlotte's and a decent age range, but not necessarily Bastien's type. And Tiffany, a younger woman with a failing candy store, who had a small daughter in need of a playmate. Despite all their faults, they were the only options left, and Charlotte had to make do with what was available.

Guilt pressed on her heart as she lied to Margot to get her here, offering a free facial and fifty bucks in exchange for her time. Margot was desperate enough that Charlotte's offer was met without hesitation. Tiffany was easy to pull in with the promise of a wedding job. Charlotte offered to purchase boxed chocolates to sweeten the deal if Tiffany would meet with her and bring some samples. Tilly would prove a tougher task. She wasn't one to wear makeup or indulge in facials. Nothing appealed to her like retro baking equipment. So, Charlotte would spin a crafty story about getting rid of her mother's antique collection and promise Tilly first dibs on any items of interest. By week's end, Charlotte hoped she would have filled the open position.

The sound of tires on gravel sent her heart racing. Bastien had returned from taking Ivy to school. She didn't know why the thought of him sent her heart aflutter each time. It could have been the way he filled a cotton shirt or his jeans for that matter, but it seemed to be more than that. She liked him and that made finding him a wife even harder.

She would have volunteered for the job herself, but she'd never get married for money. If she were ever going to walk down the aisle, it would be for love.

She watched the seconds drag by as she forced down her tea, anticipation knotting in her stomach. Would Bastien arrive in a slick suit and tie, or downplay his success and appear in her favorite jeans and black T-shirt? Her heart rate spiked as she imagined the possibilities, and when the door opened, she rose with a rush of anticipation.

Bastien stepped through the door, and Charlotte felt every cell in her body awaken to his presence. He had dressed to impress in a suit, white shirt, and polished shoes that shone like stars against the dark night sky. His face was freshly shaven, and his hair looked just-styled.

"You look incredible." She'd never seen him in anything that didn't look great. He could have been wearing a loincloth and bunny slippers and he'd still look like he'd just stepped out of a magazine shoot. He was built like a god, his jawline perfectly chiseled, and his eyes so blue they seemed to penetrate through you.

He smiled. "This is my uniform." He shrugged. "This is a business deal—nothing more than a business deal. I dressed accordingly."

"Shall we get started, then?" She'd made folders for all the candidates and handed him the one on top. She had pulled their social media profile pictures, printed them, and added what she knew about each candidate.

"The first contender is Margot." She glanced at the clock. "She should be here momentarily. I imagine she's taking her children to school."

Bastien's brows shot up like they were taking flight. "Did you say, children?"

Charlotte cleared her throat. "Yes, she has three."

"Geez, Charlotte. I'm not interested in opening a daycare. I just need a wife for a short period of time. Besides, involving children makes it tricky. They'll think it's real, and then what?"

That was one of Charlotte's biggest worries. "What about Ivy? She's going to think you're getting married, and then what do you tell her when it all falls apart?"

He grimaced. "I can't speak to the other children, but Ivy is smart enough to know the truth, and I'll tell it to her. She'll understand that I need to do this to keep her and not because I actually want to marry someone. Maybe we should try to find a candidate who is childless, just in case."

"We don't have the luxury of living in a perfect world. We live in this world, and we have thirteen days to make this happen. There are three candidates and two of them have children."

"But one doesn't?"

Charlotte didn't want to explain that Tilly was their last hope. Bastien scrutinized the file, his eyebrows shooting up when he saw Tilly's photo. "You have to be kidding,"

Charlotte tried her best to ignore the feeling that she was failing horribly. Tilly may not have been naturally beautiful, but she had a kind of charm that made her attractive. "You need someone who's available, and she's single, with no children," Charlotte said, forcing herself to sound enthusiastic. "Plus, she has a nice smile." Even as she spoke, Charlotte knew that Tilly rarely used that smile. She was short and stout and had zero fashion sense, but everyone in the kitchen loved her because of her honest and friendly nature. "And she can cook your pants off."

The atmosphere between them was thick with tension, as if a hundred unheard sentences fought to get out. "I'm keeping my pants on, thanks," he said.

Charlotte tried her best to compose herself, but she couldn't help the feeling of dread washing over her.

Her face flushed as she imagined Bastien consummating his marriage, and her heart splintered in two. He must have noted the look of anguish on her face, for he quickly cast his gaze downward.

"Like I said, this has nothing to do with sex. It's all for show."

Charlotte tried her best to compose herself, but she couldn't help the feeling of dread washing over her. She knew Bastien had to get married in order to secure his future, but it still stung to think of him with someone. "Yes, I understand that."

Bastien sighed. "It's just a person on my arm who can pass as my wife, so my mother can't use my bachelor status against me."

Charlotte stood up, not wanting him to see how this conversation was affecting her. She glanced at Tilly's picture once more before closing the folder. "As much as you don't want to focus on women with children, they will be the most believable match and, honestly, a built-in family is hard to beat when it comes to an environment that could be good for Ivy. Not only is she getting a mother, but siblings as well." She wasn't sure her argument was convincing, but Bastien nodded.

"Fine. We'll consider everyone."

Once again, tires crunched on gravel. "That must be Margot." Charlotte chanced a glance at Bastien and saw he had an expression of calm determination. "Let's do this." She walked to the door and opened it, finding Margot with her hand raised to knock. Dressed in her blue Kessler Resort T-shirt and black slacks, Margot looked more put together than she remembered. In her memory, Margot usually wore a lot less clothing and significantly more makeup.

"Come on in." Charlotte stood aside so Margot could enter.

Margot looked at her phone and smiled. "Will this take more than an hour? I have to be at The Kessler at ten."

"We'll be quick." She led her toward the kitchen, where she'd set the table up as if she were going to do a facial.

"Will I still get the fifty bucks if you speed through it?"

They entered the kitchen, and Margot's eyes latched onto Bastien. "Oh my, and who's this?" She made a beeline to him and ran her hand down his jacket sleeve. "I just love a man in a suit." She winked and giggled. "Love them more when they're out of the suit."

Poor Bastien looked up as if saying "save me." His eyes were screaming, "No, she's not the one," but he'd never say it out loud.

Charlotte wanted to smack Margot for being so forward, but she stepped between them and cleared her throat. "This is Bastien," she said, forcing a smile. "I think you two should get acquainted while I get the products ready." She could see by his expression that Margot would never do.

Bastien held out his hand. "Nice to meet you, Margot."

Margot shook his hand firmly and flashed him another flirtatious grin. "It's my pleasure." She trailed her fingers down his arm again in an intimate gesture before letting go.

If Margot was already dismissed, and by Bastien's hell-no expression, she was, then Charlotte would have to go with the ruse and give her the facial and fifty bucks.

Charlotte quickly moved to set up for the facial, putting some distance between them. She silently cursed herself for getting into this awkward situation. She knew from the beginning that this was going to be a problem.

"So, what brings you here, Bastien?" Margot asked, bringing Charlotte back from her self-flagellation to the present moment.

"My sister Chloe, who recently passed, lived next door. I've been coming here frequently." He paused and Charlotte felt his gaze linger, as if he wanted to say something else. "Charlotte and I have become close ... friends." He paused after the word "close" for an eternity, conveying a completely different meaning before finishing with "friends."

Margot jokingly pushed Charlotte's shoulder. "You're keeping him a secret!"

Charlotte didn't know what to say; she had no desire to be the subject of gossip, but she was secretly pleased that Margot believed she and Bastien could actually be together. She quickly jumped in to diffuse the situation. "Oh no, we're—"

"Private people," Bastien said with a firm nod.

Margot crossed her arms and pouted. "Not me. If I had someone like him ... I'd parade them all over town like a 4H prized pig."

Charlotte couldn't help but chuckle at the image of Bastien being paraded around town. She sensed the tension between them and knew that she needed to lighten the mood before things got too awkward. "Let's get started on that facial, shall we?"

Charlotte could feel Bastien's eyes on her as she slathered green goo on Margot's face. She imagined he was questioning her ability to do the job. Hell, she was starting to think she couldn't.

Eventually she finished up Margot's facial and paid her the fifty bucks and walked her to the door. "Let me know what you think about the product," Charlotte said.

Before Margot left, she said. "If you don't nab that one soon, someone else will."

Charlotte knew that to be certain. Within two weeks, someone was going to nab Bastien, even if it was a charade.

With a final wave goodbye, Margot left the house, leaving Charlotte and Bastien alone once again.

Bastien silently watched as Charlotte put away all of her products before speaking up. "And you thought she was a viable candidate?"

"We don't have much time to work with, so our options are limited. Besides, you said you'd marry The Statue of Liberty. At least Margot has a pulse."

"To her, I'm just meat ready to be auctioned at the 4H."

"Well, to you, she's just a hired wife. What does it matter as long as she says yes?"

He closed his eyes and took several breaths. "It has to be believable. My mom might think I found her on the corner and hired her for a night, but she'd never believe I'd marry her forever."

"Pity you wouldn't answer any of my questions yesterday."

"What do you want to know?"

She picked up her now-cold tea and emptied her mug. Men were so damn frustrating. "Bastien, the horses have already left the barn. We have two more options. Let's hope you can saddle one of them."

CHAPTER EIGHTEEN

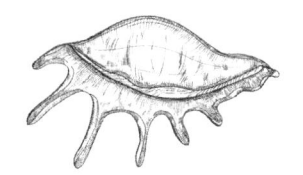

"Ivy, we're going to be late." Bastien slathered peanut butter on a bagel and added sliced bananas and wheat germ. "Breakfast is ready." He looked up some quick breakfast ideas and made this, hoping Ivy would like it. All she wanted lately was Cocoa Puffs and chocolate milk, and each time he let her have it, he was certain social services would break through the door and arrest him for bad parenting.

"I'm coming," she called out from her room. A moment later, she raced into the kitchen wearing green leggings and a pink tutu. He took her in from head to toe. At least she had the matching socks and an actual pair of shoes on today. Yesterday she insisted on wearing one boot and one sneaker. When he asked why, she told him she wanted to be prepared for anything. He couldn't argue with her logic, even though he wanted to. Her fashion sense could be best described as Annie Oakley meets Picasso, but he embraced her confidence and supported her individuality. He was pretty positive she'd grow out of her Pippi Longstocking phase.

"Try this." He cut the bagel into four pieces and put them on a plate. She ate while he attempted to tame her hair. She always asked for braids, but the most she got was a ponytail. Even that was a challenge, and he failed more often than not. Her hair looked like a bird's nest around the edges. She often appeared like she'd been caught in a windstorm, her mop going in every direction.

"Today is show and tell day."

He remembered when he was a kid and had to bring something in for show and tell. He always felt anxious, worrying if what he'd brought was good enough or if the other kids would make fun of him. Looking back, he had to admit his collection of bug carcasses had not excited his classmates or his teacher the way he thought it would.

He looked at Ivy and smiled. "What are you going to bring with you?"

She paused mid-bite, carefully set down her bagel, and picked up her sparkly, rainbow-striped unicorn backpack. She fumbled around, shaking the bag until she found what she was looking for—a small glass jar, the kind that held baby food. She pulled it out, holding it up high to show off the inside: countless multicolored shells clung together, each looking as if it had been carefully chosen. A smile spread across her face. "I promised Mommy I'd keep filling this jar full of pretty shells," she said.

"That's a wonderful plan," Bastien said, though a part of him felt sadness as he realized it would be necessary to find new ways to keep Ivy connected to her mother as time passed and memories of Chloe faded. He knew it was important that her memory lived on.

She took a bite of the bagel and sipped her milk. "Do they have seashells in New York?"

Since there were beaches nearby, he could assume there

were seashells. It wouldn't be difficult to reach a beach, but it wouldn't be as easy as her doorstep, where she could step outside and collect them. "We'll need to drive to one," he answered.

She glanced in his direction, and he could see the resemblance to Chloe in her expression. Losing Chloe would always hurt, but she lived on in her daughter, and Bastien was never more grateful to have Ivy there as a reminder that his sister had lived. "Will we have to move?"

He wasn't sure how to respond. "Not right now," he replied.

She smiled. "I don't want to leave. Charlotte is here, and so are Cricket's chocolate chip pancakes!"

He didn't want to crush her enthusiasm and say she could find pancakes anywhere, but she was right about one thing—Charlotte would never be in New York.

The days had evaporated since he'd come to Willow Bay. His life had changed so drastically that keeping his head from spinning was hard. A week ago, he was a bachelor, and now he had taken on the responsibility of caring for Ivy and was looking for a wife.

Ivy had inherited her mother's tenacity and could be quite headstrong at times, but she also possessed an inner wisdom beyond her years that often surprised him.

"Ready to go, little bug?"

She nodded and then raced to the bathroom to brush her teeth. He would have never thought of that, but someone had instilled the good habit in her, and he was grateful. He'd gone on Amazon and looked for child-rearing books. There were hundreds, maybe thousands. He knew of the *What to Expect When You're Expecting* books, but they didn't have one called *What to Expect When a Five-year-old Lands in Your Life*. He'd purchased everything he could find on raising good humans, and accidentally chose one on puppies because of the small girl on the cover. It might come in handy someday.

"Ready." She pulled on her knapsack. It wasn't the mini kind made for little ones, but a full-size backpack that could be used for hiking that hung to the back of her thighs. If filled, it would weigh more than she did.

Since that day at the airport, she'd never asked to ride in the front seat again. He was glad that wasn't going to be a constant battle. Ivy climbed into her booster in the back seat, and he buckled her up before climbing into the driver's seat and heading out.

As they passed Charlotte's house, he wondered what she was up to today. It had been a day since their disastrous first attempt at securing a bride-to-be. He couldn't blame her. He'd given her so little to go with. His only prerequisite was that the woman had to breathe and stand erect. Margot fits that qualification. He certainly had to elevate his expectations, or Charlotte might just marry him to a pig in lipstick and a wedding dress.

He and Ivy pulled up to the school, and he walked her to the entrance, holding her close. He looked into her eyes, and he whispered, "I love you." Charlotte had always taken her, and he didn't realize how weirdly emotional dropping a child at school could be.

When he returned to the house, he found Charlotte standing by the water's edge. She picked up a rock and flung it into the water.

"Good morning?"

She spun around and slapped her hand to her heart. "You scared me."

"You've got quite an arm. What's with the rock throwing?"

She shrugged and smiled. "It's just something I do every day." She shifted on her feet and then smiled. "It's silly."

"Tell me."

"How about I show you?" She pulled a permanent marker from her pocket and held it in the air. "Find something you want to return to the sea."

"Like anything?"

She cocked her head. "Well, I've always believed it should have come from there first. I threw a piece of coral back, so maybe look for a shell or something like that."

He scoured the beach before them and found a broken sand dollar. "How about this?"

"Nice one."

"Now make a wish on it." She handed him the pen. "You might need to use shorthand or numbers to remember."

"What do you do?"

"I've got thousands of wishes floating out there. I use numbers, and I'm up to five figures."

He couldn't believe that she'd been keeping track of her wishes for all that time. He wrote the number 1 on the sand dollar and handed her back her pen. "What's next?"

Charlotte smiled and nodded. "It's simple. You close your eyes and throw it in with every ounce of hope and belief that your wish will come true."

He followed her instructions, wishing to give Ivy a happier childhood and life than he had then throwing the sand dollar into the waves. When he opened his eyes again, Charlotte was smiling at him with admiration in her eyes.

"You're a good man," she said. "Ivy is lucky to have you."

His heart warmed at her words, and he felt his lips twitch into a smile as he thought about how far they'd come since Chloe passed away. It was challenging, but they were getting back on their feet again, finding joy in small moments like this one.

He took her hand in his and squeezed it gently before looking up at the sky. At that moment, he didn't care about any of his fears or anxieties; all he wanted was to appreciate life's beauty in this moment with Charlotte by his side.

"How do you know whether your wish was granted?"

"I suppose if it comes true, then it was." She laughed. "When I was little, I thought that if the item washed ashore again, the universe was watching out for me, but I was too young to understand anything about tides. If my wishes are washing on shore, they're probably showing up in New Orleans."

"What kind of things do you wish for?"

She shook her head. "I can't tell you because they may not come true."

"Have any of them come true?"

"I guess my life isn't too bad, so something's going right."

He was astonished that she'd maintained such a positive attitude despite what had transpired over the past few days. "How can you be so cheerful when you have nothing left?"

"It's not gone yet," she said before striding towards the house. "Besides, helping you make sure Ivy can have a happy life is helping me with mine. Would you like some coffee?"

"I'd love some." He trailed her inside and passed the coffee table overflowing with her trinkets. On closer inspection, he spotted more than seashells. There was jewelry, coins that had been mostly worn away, and a large glass buoy at the center of the display. It was hollowed out, filled with sand and unlit candles.

Charlotte moved around the kitchen, gathering coffee

mugs, creamer, and sugar. Once everything was on the table, she sat and pointed to the chair beside her.

"How's Ivy?"

"She's great." He took the seat. "I got her to eat something other than chocolate cereal for breakfast." He was proud of that. He'd mastered toasting bagels. He might try pigs in a blanket next.

"Sounds like you're adapting to fatherhood well."

"If I can figure out the hair situation, I'll be set." He took a sip of his coffee. It had a bitter taste that he loved. "Chicory?"

She nodded. "It's an acquired taste."

"I love it."

She put a teaspoon of sugar in her cup and gave it a splash of cream. "How can I help? On occasion, I have hair issues of my own."

He stared at her beautiful long blonde locks and wondered what they might feel like in his hands or across his bare chest. "I don't think I've seen you with a hair out of place. Do you know how to braid? Ivy loves braids. I can barely get the things around to make a ponytail."

Charlotte smiled and nodded. "Poor Ivy. Poor you. Come here. I'll show you. It's a lot easier than you think." She turned, so her back was to him, and ran her hands through her hair, separating it into three sections. He carefully studied each movement, while avoiding any of his earlier thoughts, as she showed him how to start the braid. "See, you just fold one over the other, being careful not to make it too tight."

"Your turn," she said.

After a few attempts, he got the hang of it, and soon enough, he had finished braiding Charlotte's hair. He wanted to mess it up just so he could run his fingers through her silky strands, but he didn't.

She reached up and touched the braid, then turned around with a satisfied expression. "Not bad," she said with a laugh. "Not bad at all."

He smiled back, feeling proud of himself for learning something new in the foreign land of girldom. His gaze was fixed on Charlotte's beautiful smile, and as his eyes moved to meet hers, he allowed his hand to touch her soft face and then leaned in to brushed his lips lightly against her mouth. He didn't know why he felt compelled to do it, but it felt right.

Charlotte's eyes widened, and before she could pull back, he moved closer. The kiss deepened as they abandoned themselves into the moment, their emotions swirling around them. She tasted like sunshine and honey, and he found it impossible to pull away from her soft lips and her gentle embrace. Everywhere they touched—their chests, their mouths, her hands gripping his arms—was heat, a fiery passion that coiled around him, making him want to stay there forever, even if he went up in flames.

When he gradually pulled away, Charlotte looked at him with what appeared to be a mix of embarrassment and confusion, but also burning in her eyes was passion.

"Oh my," she said, gathering herself and catching her breath. "That was a wonderful kiss, but why?"

"Because I couldn't help myself. You are amazing, resourceful, creative, smart, and so giving. You are also beautiful, and it just felt so right. I hope I didn't overstep." He was always in control, but something about Charlotte made him want to throw caution to the wind. She brought out a spontaneity and impetuousness in him he knew was always there, but no one had ever succeeded in coaxing it out of him. An idea struck him. "What if you married me?"

She nervously bit her lip and took a step back, averting her gaze from his. "I can't do that, Bastien," she said softly.

"Why not?" he said with a gentle shrug. "The bonus would come in handy, wouldn't it? The money has to be useful," he said, meaning to be a little playful, but wanting to acknowledge it would still be a business arrangement.

"That would make me like your mother, wouldn't it? She squandered her dreams on a loveless marriage simply to stay in the lifestyle she's accustomed to." Her fists were balled tight at her sides as she looked away.

"But that's not what it would be with us. We know going in that this isn't a lifetime match. It's a business arrangement with the perk that we like each other, and Ivy loves you."

She turned to face him. "Which almost makes it seem worse. I've held out for love my whole life, through the guys who only cared that I was a beauty queen to adorn their egos, to the lovely but boring ones who offered security instead of passion and adventure. No, I've come this far in my years. I'd rather live my dreams alone than marry without love—even for beautiful little Ivy, who will still be yours and not mine when the 'business arrangement,' as you describe it, is over. Your commitment to Ivy is noble, Bastien, and I'm fully committed to help you meet it, for both your sakes, but I can't be your pretend bride. Let's stick to the business arrangement we have."

She picked up her mug and pointed to the folder on the table. "Let's talk about someone who can fix your problem." She lifted her coffee mug and gestured at the folder. "Tiffany will be here at ten tomorrow. I think she might be the one."

Bastien wanted to trust her, but a part of him was not letting go of Charlotte or the kiss that still quaked through his mind and body in a way that caused him to question everything he ever believed about love. He couldn't say he was falling in love, partly because he had always guarded himself against it, but he knew the feeling was more than just a passing attraction.

CHAPTER NINETEEN

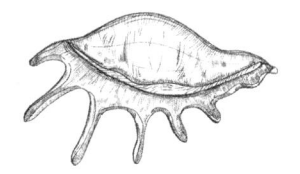

Charlotte had the wildest dream. In it, she and Bastien were standing on the beach, hand in hand. She was wearing a pair of white clam diggers with sparkling crystals sewn at the hem, and he was dashing in his black tuxedo. The waves lapped at their feet as a warm summer breeze blew through their hair. They were getting married.

The officiant spoke, but it wasn't the words that mattered. What mattered was how the two of them looked at each other and how their love filled the air with an almost tangible warmth. The officiant stopped talking, and they kissed, and that was when she woke up with her heart pounding.

She wasn't sure what was more upsetting. Was it that she'd probably never marry, and those heart-racing moments would be forever relegated to dreams, or was it because she was wearing short white pants to her wedding? No Southern girl in their right mind would settle for clam diggers, certainly not her. She had a reputation to uphold, and if she aspired to be the premiere planner in southern

Texas, she couldn't even dream of clam diggers, no matter how cutely embellished they were.

She climbed out of bed and showered but couldn't get the dream out of her head. Even her lips tingled from the kiss that didn't happen, or maybe they were still feeling the kiss that did. She hadn't been kissed like that in years.

"Oh, who are you kidding?" she asked aloud as she applied her foundation. "You've never been kissed like that." She'd read about toe-curling kisses, but she hadn't ever experienced one. She finished her makeup and pulled her hair into a messy bun. She didn't have the time to doll herself up today. She had a bride to find and a groom to satisfy.

Charlotte tried to push away the thought, but it caused her stomach to churn. She dressed in a nautical outfit, a blue and white shirt with anchors and navy-blue slacks. If she was steering this ship, she might as well dress like the captain. But why did she have this feeling that she wanted to run it all aground?

Less than an hour before Tiffany arrived, Charlotte made coffee and tidied her home. She walked out to the beach and picked up a stone. After putting a number on it, she tossed it in the water.

"What's today's wish?" a voice said from behind her.

She spun around to find Bastien. Today he wasn't in his suit but dressed in jeans and a blue Henley, slightly darker than his eyes. Dressed up or down, the man was a human form of art.

"I can't tell you, or it won't come true."

He bent over and picked up a small conch shell. They rarely showed up fully intact, and if it were her, she'd have put it on her table with all her other treasures, but maybe it would bring Bastien a special wish, so she said nothing and watched him wind up and toss it back into the sea.

"Do you want to know what I wished for?"

She did, but she wouldn't ask. "It's your wish, Bastien."

He stared at the water. "Nope, I gave this one to you. I wished that you'd get whatever you need in your life."

Charlotte smiled and sighed. "You are kind and generous."

"I'm not sure about being kind, but as far as generous ... money is all I have to offer."

She was shocked to hear him say that. "Not true." She wanted to tell him he was handsome, but that wasn't what a person should focus on. She loathed it when men saw her beauty first. Maybe that's what made Bastien different. He saw her for the person she was. He told her she was resourceful, creative, smart, and giving. He mentioned her beauty, but it came last.

"You have a big heart. You're conscientious, responsible, patient, and loving. You're also handsome." She smiled and lowered her head. "And you kiss like a porn star."

Bastien let out a soft chuckle. "Have you been kissed by porn stars often?"

Charlotte played in the sand with the toe of her shoe. "No," she replied, "but you kiss like I imagine one would."

He stepped closer to her and gently brushed a rogue strand of hair from in front of her eyes. His gaze never leaving hers, he bent his head down and pressed his lips to hers in a tender yet passionate kiss. She felt herself melting into him as his hands moved to cup her face and then around her waist as he pulled her closer.

Eventually, they broke apart, but neither seemed willing to let go. Instead, they stayed there, gazing into one another's eyes as if searching for something more than a physical connection.

Bastien cleared his throat and said, "I think we should get back inside before Tiffany arrives." He smiled softly and grabbed her hand, leading them back up the beach toward Charlotte's house.

A shadow passed them, and Bastien turned to look at the man who'd appeared on the beach.

"Isn't that the guy from the diner? The loss prevention consultant?"

Bastien's eyes narrowed, and his body stiffened. "That's no consultant. I'd bet my money he's a private eye."

"What?"

"Stay here," Bastien said as he squared his shoulders. "I'm going to talk with him."

Charlotte watched as Bastien walked towards the stranger on the beach. She couldn't hear what they were saying, but it appeared as if the conversation quickly turned confrontational, with both men standing in tense stances with voices raised. Moments later, Bastien pulled something out of his pocket and handed it to the man. They shook hands, and Bastien walked away, pulling out his phone and punching a number.

As the man walked between the two houses back toward his car, he stopped in front of her porch. "You've got yourself a good man there."

"Oh, he's ..." She was about to say he wasn't hers, but she didn't finish her sentence. She had no idea what had transpired between the two, but something had. "Yes, he's a good man." That statement felt true, down to her core. "Are you actually a loss prevention consultant?"

He laughed. "Are any of us who we say we are?" He disappeared around the corner of her house. She heard an engine roar and saw a black SUV leave the side of the road.

She had five minutes before Tiffany arrived. The thought made her insides twist, but that was because Bastien had kissed her again, and now she felt like the other woman.

She'd set out three mugs for coffee when a soft knock sounded at the door. Charlotte opened it to find Tiffany dressed in black slacks and a white blouse that seemed to hug and enhance her breasts. A surge of jealousy ribboned through her.

Tiffany held up a pink and brown box with a smirk. Sweet on You, the candy store she owned in town, had seen better days. It was no secret that her ex had bought the building and purposely raised the rent to try to control her. He'd keep the rent steady, as long as he thought he had a chance to win her back, but everyone knew her heart wasn't in it; she loved the shop, but not him.

She opened the door wider and invited Tiffany in. "Thanks for bringing those," she said politely. Tiffany nodded and followed her into the kitchen.

Another knock sounded at the door, and Bastien stuck his head in and called out, "Can I come in?"

"Yes," Charlotte said, peeking her head through the doorway. "We're in here."

Charlotte noticed the uneasiness in Bastien's demeanor and wondered what had transpired on the call. "Are you okay?" she whispered as he entered the kitchen.

"Yeah, I'm fine," Bastien said with a tight-lipped smile. He sat at the kitchen table across from Tiffany and uncharacteristically avoided eye contact.

"Tiffany, this is Bastien. Bastien, this is Tiffany."

"It's nice to meet you," Bastien said as he shook her

hand. He then returned his attention to the box on the table. "You brought samples?"

Tiffany looked at Charlotte with a thousand questions in her eyes. She hadn't told Tiffany there would be anyone else meeting them. She didn't know they were going to spring a proposition on her. She was like a sheep walking into a lion's den.

"Bastien is the client."

Tiffany sat up and smiled. "Oh, that's lovely. Let me show you what I brought." She opened the box to reveal an array of decadent confections from Sweet on You.

Tiffany's gaze shifted back to Charlotte. "Where's the bride?"

Charlotte took a deep breath and gathered her courage. This was the moment of truth.

"Well, here's the thing," she said. "We're in a bit of a pickle." Charlotte gave her the short version about Chloe's death, Ivy, and the impending custody battle.

Tiffany frowned. "And where do I come in?"

Bastien cleared his throat. "I was hoping you'd be the bride."

Tiffany's jaw dropped, looking from Bastien to Charlotte in disbelief. She opened her mouth to speak, but no words came out.

Charlotte stepped in and placed a comforting hand on Tiffany's arm. "It's a difficult situation, and we understand if you don't want to get involved. We wouldn't ask you if it wasn't necessary," she said.

Bastien nodded and added, "If you agree, you will be handsomely rewarded for your time."

"Let me get this straight. You want me to marry you?"

Bastien grimaced. "I want you to pretend to marry me. We don't actually have to walk down the aisle."

"No," Charlotte broke in. "It can be as easy as clam diggers on the beach." She didn't know why she blurted it out. Saying it out loud made it even worse. "Oh, I almost forgot." She pulled a non-disclosure agreement from a nearby folder and slid it in front of Tiffany. "I should have asked for this first."

Bastien chuckled. "Remind me not to put you in charge of any top-secret deals."

Charlotte lifted her shoulders with a shrug. "It's not like she won't sign it." She hoped she was right. "You'll sign it, right?"

Tiffany glanced down at the form. "What is it?"

Charlotte sighed. "It just says that you won't repeat anything you heard in this room."

Tiffany took the pen and scribbled her name on the signature line. "No one would believe it, anyway."

"So, what do you think?" Bastien asked.

"I think you're nuts." Tiffany stared at Bastien. "No offense, but you're so much older than me. What will people think?"

"That you're marrying me for my money. It's believable. I have a lot of money."

"I'm not a marry-for-money kind of girl. I didn't even know my ex had money until after I said, 'I do.' I'm more of a bum magnet." Her cheeks turned red. "Until I met Cormac, but I can't be with him until I get rid of my ex, and that's impossible when you have a kid together." Her expression softened. "Ava is the best thing that came out of my marriage."

Charlotte thought it was a good omen that Tiffany hadn't stood and stomped out.

Bastien took a piece of chocolate and popped it into his mouth. "You'd have Ivy's vote."

At the mention of Ivy, Charlotte smiled. She was head over heels in love with her. But if Tiffany said yes, then Ivy would be spending more time with Tiffany, which made her heart ache.

"I'll leave you two to get to know each other better."

She picked up her phone, walked out of the house, and immediately dialed Emmaline. "I need to ask you a hypothetical question."

"Is this a question related to why you're hanging out with Bastien Richmond all the time?"

She could lie to her friend, but she didn't need to. "He needs a wife to ensure he can keep custody of Ivy."

"And you said yes?"

"Of course not. I'll only marry for love."

"And what is he offering?"

The last they talked, he was offering a hundred grand. It was a fortune to nearly anyone but a rounding error to him. He had told her he'd spend far more if he entered a lengthy court battle. She imagined he was right.

"A hundred grand."

"Do you have to sleep with him?"

"No," she said with more disappointment coloring her voice than she intended.

"Girl, put away your Cinderella story fantasies. A man is offering you a hundred grand to be his pretend wife. You don't have to clean his house, do his laundry, or have his children. Most wives get far less and have to give so much more. You need the money to rebuild Because You Said Yes. You won't have to wait on the insurance; whatever they pay, you can tuck that away for a nest egg. You can be sitting pretty in no time."

Charlotte didn't want to tell her friend that a hundred

grand merely scratched the surface of what she needed. It would at least save her from losing her house.

"You're right, but Em, nowhere in all my childhood fantasies did I think I'd say yes to money instead of the man."

"He's a looker."

"Hollywood handsome."

"Cricket likes him, and that's saying something. She pretends to like everyone but likes no one."

"He's a good man."

There was a moment of silence before Emmaline laughed. "Oh my God. You're falling in love with him."

"I'm not," she lied.

"You are, and that little girl is just icing on your wedding cake."

There was no use lying. "He's amazing, Em, but he doesn't love me. This is all business; if I married him, I'd want so much more."

She walked along the beach and found a small conch shell tumbling in the waves. If she didn't know better, she would have thought it was the one Bastien had tossed into the water. She picked it up and remembered what he had said. "Even he wants me to have whatever I need." Bastien didn't wish for her to have everything she wanted. He asked the universe to give her everything she needed.

"What are you going to do?"

Charlotte exhaled deeply, letting go of all her hopes and dreams, and inhaled the possibilities of her future if she had reasonable expectations.

"I'm going to say yes. But don't tell anyone. Promise?"

"I promise."

"It may not even get to the wedding. Maybe we can pretend to be engaged."

Emmaline laughed. "Girl, think like a businesswoman. He'll pay for the wedding, and you're the planner. *Kaching. Kaching.* Besides, I've got something used since your fantasy dress was destroyed. Then again, I'm sure he can afford to buy you something new. We'll work on the borrowed and blue."

Charlotte supposed if it got to that point, what she wore wouldn't matter. She could probably get away with last night's dream attire. "I've got to go." She hung up and headed back into the house, ready to tell Bastien she'll be his wife.

She found him and Tiffany standing in the kitchen, shaking hands.

Bastien turned to Charlotte. "I'd like you to meet my fiancée, Tiffany Townsend."

Charlotte's stomach dropped, and she stumbled back. Tears started forming, but she didn't dare let them fall. "I'm overjoyed," she said, but her voice shook as she swiped at her eyes. She moved forward, her legs feeling like lead. She wanted to scream at the unfairness in the world and run away, but all she could do was stand there, smile, and face the consequences of her actions. She'd brought them together, fully expecting this result. It had never occurred to her that success would hurt so much.

CHAPTER TWENTY

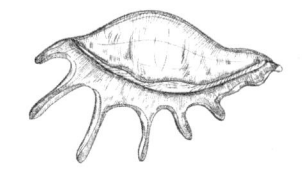

Bastien felt unsettled and conflicted about the deal he had made with Tiffany. He knew it solved his problem, but it felt off. It was harder to override his integrity than he expected, but what choice did he have? The woman who might have made him an honest man turned him down flat. He asked Charlotte to take care of the contract and left to take care of days of unanswered emails. It had been three days since he and Charlotte had been together, and he missed her more than he'd imagined possible. He had asked her for dinner, but she declined, saying she was too exhausted. He had gone to the beach in front of her house, hoping to see her make a wish on the ocean, but only the memory of his own wishes was there. Early this morning, he heard a car start up and rushed outside, hoping it was her. The silver vehicle was slowly driving away, but Charlotte never once turned around to look back.

He stared at his phone, ready to text her, but it rang before he could dial her number. His mother's name flashed across the screen. He hadn't spoken to her since the tumultuous confrontation with her private investigator. He debated answering now, but knew if he didn't, she'd call everyone at her disposal to track him down. Last year when he avoided her calls at Christmastime, she sent the police to do a welfare check. She was a bloodhound on the trail.

He lifted the receiver to his ear, bracing himself for a barrage of questions and reprimands. "Hello, Mother."

"I hope you're doing well, dear," she said. "Ivy too?" To his surprise, her voice was soft and gentle.

Bastien let out a slow breath. "All's well here. Ivy is fine. More than fine. She's happy."

"I'm not asking only about Ivy. I'm asking about you, too." He flopped onto the couch, pulling the phone from his ear to check the caller ID and make sure it was his mother. Since when did she care how he was doing?

"I'm good. Busy as usual." He wanted to slap his forehead for saying that because his business was one of his mother's chief concerns when it came to caring for Ivy.

"Have you found another nanny?"

It had been three days since he'd paid the private eye to leave. Loyalty was important to some, but money spoke to most, and all he had to do was pay more than his mother to get the man to go away.

"I'm sure your guy reported that I still don't have help."

She paused for a beat. "That's why I'm calling. Raising a child is exhausting. I should know. I had two."

He didn't want to point out that she hadn't raised either, as they were having a civil conversation, so he ignored her comment. "Ivy is an easy kid," he said. "She's no trouble at all. Chloe did an amazing job. Ivy makes great choices." Most of the time, he felt like Ivy was the mature one and he was the kid. She was teaching him so much about hope, resilience, generosity of spirit, and love. Recently, she'd come home with only half of the shells she'd brought for show and tell. When he asked her what happened to them, she said she thought it would be better to make it a share-and-tell day. He knew how important those shells were to her, and when he asked if she'd miss them, she smiled and said yes, but it was like sharing a part of her mom with everyone else, and that made her feel like she was there.

He had a feeling his mother wasn't phoning to chat. "What is the reason for your call, Mother?" he asked. She never called without a motive, and they were far from being friends who just chatted to catch up.

His mother cleared her throat before saying, "Yes, the conductor for the philharmonic got the flu, so they moved the show to next month. I'll be arriving tomorrow afternoon." His mother's reply sent his heart into free fall. He'd just managed to acquire a suitable pretend fiancée but had no idea who she was. There was no way they would survive an Annette Richmond cross-examination.

"Tomorrow? Where will you stay?"

"With you, of course."

He ground his teeth together. "No, that won't work," he said firmly. "You should try The Kessler. We don't have enough bedrooms here—they're both taken." It wasn't exactly a lie; the house had three bedrooms, one of which was empty. He thought about converting it into an office for the time being.

"You're going to send your mother to a hotel?"

"It's a resort, mother. You'll probably like it." It wasn't the Four Seasons, but it would do. "They have housekeepers, staff, and room service. You'll feel right at home."

"Alright, I'll make the call," she said. "It would be great if we could be friendly, for Ivy's sake."

He wanted to say, "Then stop being such a jerk," but he held his tongue. "It would be better for all of us if we could get along, not just Ivy. Chloe didn't want this. Ivy doesn't want this, and if you search your heart, you know you don't want this either." He hated to bring it up, but age was an issue. "You'll be eighty-eight when she graduates from high school. You're too old to raise a child."

"But I don't look a day over fifty."

He had to admit that his mother was youthful looking, but she'd had a lot of work done. He knew that she'd had multiple plastic surgeries over the years, from facelifts to Botox injections, and he couldn't help but wonder if her pursuit of youth was worth it. It was a lot of pain and money to delay something that would catch up to her in the end.

"I'd like to see Ivy for dinner tomorrow. Where can we meet?"

The only place he knew was the diner. "Cricket's at five."

"Bring your fiancée. I can't wait to meet her."

Well, shit. With the recent developments, his timeline had been drastically shortened. He needed to talk to Tiffany.

"Sure thing. See you tomorrow."

He ended the call and adjusted his schedule. He snatched his keys and drove into town to explain to Tiffany that his mother had altered their plans. He had assumed they had some time before Tiffany was required to step up, but his mother's interference had compressed time once again.

He arrived at Sweet on You and found Tiffany behind the counter.

"Hello, honey." She smiled sweetly. "Is there another name I should call you? What about snookums?" she teased.

"Only call me that if you don't want me to answer." His

voice was more serious than he had intended, but he was in no mood for jokes.

"What's going on?"

"My mother is arriving early, which means we have to speed up the plan," he said with a sigh. "She wants to meet you."

Tiffany's eyes widened. "Tonight?"

He shook his head. "No, tomorrow for dinner."

She bit her lip, looking slightly worried. "Okay, but we haven't had time to go over anything. What do I need to know?"

"Just pretend to be shy and follow my lead." There wasn't enough time to go over the things they needed to know about each other. "I'll guide you."

"What about Ava?"

From what she told him, her daughter was three and not a big talker, so he didn't see her coming along as a problem. He hadn't had time to talk to Ivy about much. The truth was, he didn't know how to speak to her about a ruse, a lie. He knew he should teach her the importance of truth and honesty, but this charade was unavoidable, for her own sake. "Come early, and we'll introduce the kids and go from there. I'll see you tomorrow."

The bell above the door sounded, and in strutted an imposing man with an air of superiority that suggested he thought he owned the place.

Bastien turned away, but the man in a gray T-shirt and jeans stepped in front of the door. "What do you mean, you'll see her tomorrow?" His voice was low and menacing. His eyes locked with Bastien's, and his hands clenched into fists.

"Let him go, Marcus." Tiffany's face peeked over the

counter, fear, and determination in her hazel eyes. "It's got nothing to do with you."

Bastien told him to step aside, but Marcus was not budging. "Not until you explain why my wife is meeting up with you tomorrow," he said.

"Ex-wife," Tiffany snapped. She grabbed the phone. "I'm calling the police."

"I haven't done anything yet," Marcus said.

Bastien didn't like the sound of the word "yet." It always implied more to come, and he had more than enough on his plate. The man was far enough away from Tiffany that he'd have to go through Bastien first to harm her. That was a small consolation under the circumstances.

"What's your business with Tiffany?" Marcus asked.

Bastien stood firm. "It's none of your business." He wasn't stupid enough to tell the man anything. He stared down at Marcus's ham hock fists and took a step back.

"We're wedding planning," Tiffany yelled. "Now leave."

After talking to Tiffany the other day, he considered her to be intelligent, but that was the poorest move ever. Did she think saying anything about a wedding would calm this guy's obvious jealous rage? He opened his mouth to speak, but Marcus's fist landed on his jaw before he could form a word. So much for diffusing the situation. It was all Bastien could do to restrain himself from knocking the aggressor to the floor, but Tiffany was still in no danger and hitting back would constitute a fight that would land him in equal trouble. His mother would have a heyday in court with that.

At least Tiffany had been smart enough to call 911 at the outset. The next hour passed in a blur of police reports, cold compresses, and Tiffany's deep regret. At least they wouldn't have to worry about Marcus for the time being, since he would be kept in jail until his bond hearing.

He now missed Charlotte even more and took a stroll along the street, hoping he'd find her, or they'd meet by chance. Unfortunately, her shop was empty. He walked down the street to Cricket's and took a seat precisely underneath a framed image of a rooster swinging with the words "Fowl Play" beneath it. The irony wasn't lost on Bastien when he looked up and saw the image.

"What happened to you?" Cricket asked as she came closer. She examined his bruised and slightly swollen jaw. "Wow. It looks like Charlotte put a hurtin' on you." She snickered. "I didn't know she could be so tough."

He winced and clamped his hand against his aching jaw. "It wasn't Charlotte." He massaged the tender area. "Have you seen her?"

"She was in here earlier fighting with the insurance adjuster. They refuse to compensate her because of a lack of photographic evidence. It appears they think she is trying to pull something over on them."

"But weren't there photos of the store before the damages?" he asked.

Cricket sat down opposite him. "Apparently, they can't confirm it was her shop that was damaged," she said. "She's been trying to get her friends to make statements."

"I'd be glad to provide a statement in support," he offered.

Cricket pushed back in her seat and folded her arms. "Are you two having an argument?"

Cricket's words jarred him. They weren't fighting, were they? She hadn't said a word to him since Tiffany showed up. Maybe he was too presumptuous when he kissed her a second time. He knew he had been too forward the first time, although she told him she liked it.

"I assumed you and she were a couple. She always seems so cheerful in your presence, and your daughter adores Charlotte. She's a real gem, a once-in-a-lifetime woman, and a force of nature."

"We're just friends." Those words didn't sit any better with Bastien than the agreement with Tiffany, but they were the truth no matter what else he felt.

"Do you smooch all your buddies?"

He cocked his head. "How did you know that?"

"Small-town gossip is like an emergency alert system and probably more efficient. Dr. Robinson mentioned seeing you on the beach to Agnes Myers, and once it gets to Agnes, it spreads like wildfire."

"Good to know."

"Let me give you a word of advice," Cricket said.

Bastien leaned back and waited.

"If you're looking for a good woman," she said, "you won't find anyone better than Charlotte. She's the best of the best. But if it's trouble you're chasing,"—she looked at his sore jaw—"go back to Sweet on You. Maybe you like coming out of there with a nasty bruise." She pulled out her pad. "What'll it be?"

It would appear that Cricket missed nothing in town.

"What do you suggest?"

She smiled. "I've got the perfect thing for you. How about my 'pull your head from your ass' stew? It's served with a 'just say you're sorry' salad and a big baboon biscuit." She wrote it down. "Just friends, my ass. If you can't see how Charlotte feels about you, you don't deserve her. Worse, you don't seem to wanna let yourself see how you feel about her, but I do, and I have since the first time I saw you two together."

"I don't believe in a love that lasts forever, let alone love at first sight. Charlotte feels nothing for me," he said flatly.

Cricket rolled her eyes. "Save room for the idiot ice cream dessert. Ever ask yourself what would have brought you this far in life without someone by your side if it wasn't you just waiting for the right one? You don't believe in love? Gimme a break. You just don't believe in you, except if you're wheelin' and dealin'. Any bank accounts hug you lately? Has any contract looked at you sweetly and told you everything was gonna be okay? No, that's what love does. You know what else love does? It shows up when you lose someone close and there's no one to look after a sweet, precious little girl who is counting on you for everything from chocolate chip pancakes to college. Charlotte showed up for you even when her own dreams were literally washed away. And you think she feels nothing for you? Wow, it must be dark under that rock where you live. This ain't my first rodeo, son. I know what I know. I'm going to bring you a side of 'open your eyes' cobbler with that idiot ice cream."

CHAPTER TWENTY-ONE

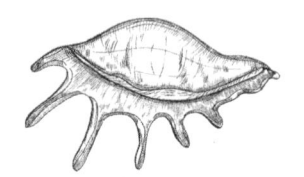

"What do you mean, you're not marrying him?"

Emmaline reached for her wine but kept rocking. Ollie's tail swished back and forth, narrowly avoiding a pinch from the chair.

After her run-in with the insurance adjuster, Charlotte headed straight for Emmaline's ranch.

"I marched back to the house to tell him I'd do it, but I was too late. They'd already made the deal." It shouldn't have come as a surprise since Bastien's career was about making deals. Although she was sure most of his deals made him money rather than cost him.

"And you didn't say anything?"

She slipped off her shoes and curled up in her chair before grabbing her glass of wine. "What could I say? It was my job to find him a wife, and I did that. He's paying me a lot of money," she said with resignation. "Hey, Honey, I changed my mind. You kissed me, and I don't want you kissing her?"

Charlotte looked out at a rolling green landscape with white fences marking the property boundaries. She could just make out a cliff edge in the distance where the sun shimmered off the bay's surface. She took in the sweeping views of far-off hills and never-ending sky that were so different from Emmaline's beach resort.

"Do you miss it?"

Em stared at her. "Miss what?"

"The Brown." Em had been filled with purpose since the day she was born. She was driven to prove she could run her family's resort, even though they had been doubtful. Charlotte was raised to be happy, but happiness didn't necessarily drive ambition. As she watched her friends grow up to become something, her only claim to fame was wearing a beauty queen crown by default and being able to take ten years off any face with her makeup tricks. That was no small task, but it didn't make her feel like she'd created something or made the world a better place. Deep down she knew her true gift was touching people's lives in ways that made them infinitely better and changed them, but she had a hard time giving herself credit for that thinking because wasn't that what everyone did?

"Oh, hell no. I thought I would, but while The Brown drove me to do something, it mostly drove me nuts. I'm glad things worked out the way they did. It took me thirty years, but I finally got what I wanted all along—Miles."

Charlotte smiled. "I'm so happy for you." And she genuinely was. Charlotte celebrated the successes of her friends as if they were her own. Jealousy and envy were not in her DNA, and she was grateful for that without realizing what a rare gift it was.

"Your fairytale ending is just within reach. All you need to do is put your Southern charm into action and go get it! Let's both admit we know you have feelings for him—will you let him slip away?"

Charlotte sighed. Fairy tales were for someone else, and they implied she needed saving. She was equal parts pragmatist and romanticist. How else could she have held out all these years without settling for less than the perfect man for her? She knew she felt something strong for Bastien, but she couldn't put a word to it—was it love? Or was it make believe? Was she making Bastien into someone or something he wasn't? The kisses were real. Holding him and him holding her was real. His loving gaze was as real as a sunrise, but his proposal was so matter of fact. Maybe it was simply admiration for all that he was doing to keep Ivy. Without a doubt, Charlotte was smitten with Ivy, but kids were easy to fall in love with. This circular dialog was making her dizzy.

"I don't know what I'm supposed to do, Em. I feel like I'm on one of those glass bridges high above a canyon where you can't tell if your next step will be another move forward or a fall deep into the abyss." Her gaze fixed on the distant horizon.

Em grinned and winked at her knowingly. "I know you well enough to know the circular conversation you're having with yourself. Stop the spin, Charlotte. Go after him! You two were made for each other. You're both scared, but if I can see how perfect you are together, you can too."

Charlotte smiled and shook her head. Was this happening? She'd known Em for years, and never once had they discussed love—at least not in any profound or meaningful way. Yet here they were, discussing matters of the heart as if Em believed Charlotte might do the unthinkable and chase after Bastien Richmond— confirmed billionaire bachelor extraordinaire who seemed uninterested in a real committed relationship. He tossed money around like he could buy anything, and it would seem that he could as she'd just procured him a fiancée and possibly a wife. What if Tiffany was the one? She had a little girl, and if Charlotte was honest, it made perfect sense to set them up. Sure, Tiffany was on the younger side, but lots of women liked older men, and Bastien didn't look even close to his age. Good genes, she imagined, because his mother looked darn good too. If everything was so perfect, why was it sitting so uncomfortably with her? The truth hit her like an oncoming train. Her heart knew what her head wouldn't admit. Bastien Richmond *was* the perfect man for her.

Charlotte drained her glass of wine before turning back to Emmaline. "It seems I'm a day late and a dollar short," she admitted softly.

"But you don't have to be," Em said decisively, refilling Charlotte's glass with more wine before pouring one for herself. "What are you so afraid of? You have to be willing to take risks when you want something badly enough." She paused before continuing, "Fear has never stopped you before. I believe in you, and I think you should go after your man!"

Charlotte couldn't help but smile at her friend's excitement. Risky or not, maybe it was time she took a chance on herself...and on Bastien too, but she needed the night to think about it.

"Can I stay over?"

Emmaline sat up and looked around their chairs. "You'll have to. Ollie's stolen your left shoe. It will take until morning to find it, anyway. And we've enjoyed too much wine for you to drive."

CHARLOTTE WOKE to a weight on her chest. She opened her eyes to find Ollie on top of her and her left shoe in his mouth.

She patted Ollie's head, took her shoe, and rolled him off her before she climbed out of bed. Today was the first day of the rest of her life. All morning, Charlotte went through the motions, trying to gather the courage she needed to face Bastien. By lunchtime, armed with Em's words of encouragement and her own determination, she stood on the weathered porch outside of Bastien's house, ready to take control of her destiny. She knocked on the door, but the sound echoed unanswered. She looked around and noticed that his car was missing and turned her attention to the shore. She hadn't made a wish for the past two days and picked up a shell to toss as an offering. It was mostly white with a pink center, and when she turned it over, she noticed the faded markings of a black pen. Four numbers were barely visible. This was an old wish, but it had been returned to her. It didn't matter what the number said, because she always wished for the same thing—a life filled with joy and happiness. She tucked the shell into her pocket, considering it a good sign, then headed back to her house. If she was going to prepare for her future, she didn't want to step into it wearing yesterday's clothes and no makeup. While Bastien's absence was disappointing, it was probably a blessing in disguise. She showered again, thinking about how Marybeth always said cleanliness was close to godliness. She had chosen her prettiest floral dress for the day and sat by the window with hopeful anticipation, watching the sun track its way across the sky. As four-thirty came and went, she felt her expectations sink as she realized Bastien wasn't coming home anytime soon.

She was desperate to find him, so she bravely ventured

into town. As she drove down Main Street, she spotted his car in front of Cricket's. Her heart raced as she searched fruitlessly for a place to park her car. With each passing moment, her anxiety grew, but her mission remained clear—she had to find him and tell him how she felt. She passed by her store but didn't stop, Because You Said Yes wasn't her priority at that moment. Besides, her shop wasn't much to look at right now. The only thing remaining was the polished concrete flooring and some drywall.

She found a parking spot in front of Sweet On You, and exited the car. She passed by a woman who looked out of place on Main Street. Dressed in what was most definitely Chanel or perhaps Valentino, she was more suited to a boardroom meeting than a stroll through Willow Bay.

Charlotte peered inside the diner's window and glimpsed Bastien and Ivy. They were both smiling and looking so happy. Ivy adored her uncle and clearly felt safe and nurtured when with him. And Bastien, of course, loved Ivy more than he ever knew possible, a love that only deepened the minute he knew she was his. As Charlotte craned her neck to see what was causing such joy, she saw Tiffany, who seemed equally cheerful.

Her heart sank with the realization that there was no future for her and Bastien. She turned to leave and heard the woman in the black dress say, "I'm telling you. That's not the girl who was kissing him. This one is younger and prettier. I told you. It's all scripted so he can keep Ivy."

At the mention of Ivy, Charlotte stopped. The woman on the phone had to be Bastien's mother, who was on to his game. In an instant, she recognized her from the brief encounter at the funeral. There was a minute of hesitation where her brain and her heart battled it out. Her brain told her to walk away and let Bastien deal with the fallout, but her heart told her to do what was right. Preserving Ivy's happiness counted the most.

She spun around and entered the diner, making a beeline straight for Tiffany and Bastien. She smiled at Bastien while Ivy crawled across her uncle to get to Charlotte.

"You're here. I missed you so much." Ivy wrapped her arms around Charlotte and held on like a vise.

"I missed you too."

She turned her attention to Tiffany. "You need to go. Bastien's mom is outside."

"Oh good, we were waiting for her," Tiffany said.

Charlotte shook her head. "No, you don't understand. She saw you, and she knows you're not the one. Take Ava and go now."

Bastien stood and looked past her, and she knew they were out of time. "I'm sorry I'm late, sweetheart. The insurance adjuster is being a thorn in my side." She wrapped her hand around the back of his head, pulled him forward, and pressed her lips to his for far longer than was decent in polite society – but it was fine in Cricket's Diner. Before she pulled away, she whispered, "Play along. Your mother is watching."

Bastien stepped back, and for a moment, he looked confused, but he snapped into action. "Hello, love." He looked her up and down. "You look so pretty today." He kissed her again. "I missed you."

"I missed you too."

Ivy, who was stuck between them, looked up. "I missed you three."

"Bastien," his mother's voice called from behind. "Do you want to introduce me to your fiancée?"

Tiffany shifted, but Bastien stood in front of where she was seated to block her view.

"Mom, this is Charlotte."

Charlotte offered her hand as Annette didn't have that give-me-a-hug look about her. "It's a pleasure to formerly meet you. I was at the funeral, and you asked who I was."

Annette stared at her. "I remember you. You didn't say anything about being Sebastian's intended then."

Charlotte pasted on a beauty queen smile. "It wasn't the right time. That was Chloe's day." She turned to Bastien. "I thought your mom was coming in later."

His eyes grew wide. "I'm sorry, it skipped my mind. We've been so busy. It feels like I haven't seen you in three days."

A warm feeling rushed through her to know that he was counting, too.

Annette looked around them at Tiffany. "And who is this?"

The door to the diner opened, and in walked Marcus Townsend. Charlotte had heard a lot about him, most of it not good. "I won't stand by while you take my wife from me," he yelled.

"Ex-wife," Tiffany said.

Charlotte knew she had to act quickly, or things would twirl out of control faster than a tornado in a teacup. "This is Tiffany. She owns Sweet on You in town, and she's making the chocolate for our wedding. She brought over some samples the other day, and I asked her to meet us here to tell her what we preferred. And we thought it would be nice for Ivy and Ava to meet."

Marcus frowned and pinned Tiffany with a look. "Wait a minute. I thought you said you were wedding planning."

She rolled her eyes. "If you paid closer attention, we might still be married. I said I was wedding planning, but not Bastien's and my wedding. It's for Charlotte and Bastien." Tiffany pointed to Charlotte. "He's got a fiancée." She rolled her eyes. "Besides, he's way too old for me." She slid out of the booth and picked up Ava before turning to Charlotte. "Just drop by tomorrow, and we'll discuss the details."

Charlotte hugged her and whispered, "Nothing for you has changed."

Tiffany laughed, hugging her back. "It looks like everything has for you, sweet Charlotte."

CHAPTER TWENTY-TWO

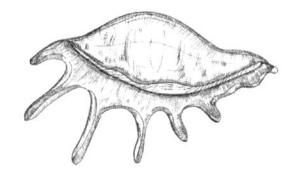

Bastien wasn't sure what was happening, but Charlotte seemed in charge. She had gone from flatly refusing his offer to marry him to storming Cricket's Diner and dispensing with the pretend bride she herself had arranged like she was sweeping a dead bug off the porch. He had never seen a deal turn around this quickly without a roomful of lawyers and both sides pressuring them to get it done. Of course, this wasn't the standard deal, or any deal at all. Something else was taking shape here. He sure hoped that she knew what she was doing. His mother had few worthy adversaries and Charlotte had just put herself between her and her goal of taking Ivy. It would not be pretty. That it didn't seem to faze Charlotte was not lost on Bastien as he appreciated this new take-no-prisoners side of her too.

He pointed to the booth and said, "Let's sit." They waited for his mother to choose a side, and the trio all crammed into the opposite bench.

"Ivy, come sit next to Mee-maw."

She was squashed in between him and Charlotte but shook her head. "No, thank you. I'm nice and warm right here."

His mother narrowed her eyes. "What have you been telling her?" She looked back to Ivy and said, "I won't bite."

Bastien wanted to laugh. Everything about his mother was worse than a bite unless you had anti-venom nearby. "Mother, Ivy just told you she is happy here. I don't need to tell her anything. She can speak for herself. I find that children and dogs are great at reading people."

Charlotte ran her hand over Ivy's braids and smiled. "Honey, you can stay here if you want, but your grandmother would love to sit by you."

Bastien wondered if Charlotte used the term grandmother intentionally, knowing his mother didn't like it. Then again, he didn't think Charlotte had a mean or spiteful bone in her body, and it was probably just an innocent remark.

Ivy clung to Charlotte for a few more minutes before she disappeared under the table to appear seconds later on the other side.

"Your hair looks lovely. Did Charlotte braid it?" Annette asked.

Ivy shook her head. "No, Uncle Bast did it, but Charlotte taught him."

His mother smiled and gave him an I-don't-believe-it look.

"It's true. It turns out you can teach an old dog new tricks." He wondered if that went for everything. Was it possible for his mother to learn how to step back and not drive everything? He hoped so. He'd been thinking a lot about her visit since the day prior and wondered if they might come to some compromise or at least lay down some healthy boundaries for him and Ivy. It would be fine for his mother to make her demands if only his life were affected, but her custody threats were turning many lives upside down. Thankfully, not Ivy's, not yet anyway. But Charlotte wouldn't come out of this unscathed. She was an innocent bystander in all of this. Then there was Tiffany, Ava, and even Marcus, who hadn't assumed incorrectly. He didn't feel too badly about him because it was clear that Marcus wasn't up for the husband of the year award. He knew the money he'd pay Tiffany would help her and Ava get away from Marcus. Maybe then Marcus would realize then he needed help for his daughter's sake.

"Penny for your thoughts," Charlotte said, her voice angelic.

Bastien chuckled. "That's a pretty low bid." The cost of his decisions and agreements since his sister's death would be expensive, but one couldn't put a value on love or Ivy's happiness. Maybe that was what was wrong with his mother. Had she ever experienced love or even the love of herself? And if she loved herself, wouldn't she have expected more from life?

He glanced at the woman across the table who had never been happy. He wished he knew how to make things better for her, to bring some joy to her existence. One thing he knew for sure, the answer wasn't to put Ivy in her care. It was obvious to him she only wanted Ivy as some sad way to fix the past with Chloe, and that would only suck the joy out of Ivy's life and make her feel responsible for her grandmother. Ivy would end up adrift and missing her mother instead of celebrating her. It was remarkable to him how Chloe managed to leave this world and yet imbue Ivy with endless joy and hope instead of fear and sadness. He would never let his mother undo that, and he knew a big part of it was riding on him fulfilling his promise.

He returned his attention to Charlotte, whose eyes were filled with concern for him and his family situation. She reached over and took his hand in hers, squeezing it softly as if to tell him everything was going to be okay. He thought about what Cricket had said earlier. She was right. No contract or bank account had ever made him feel safe or loved. And no one had moved him or protected him the way Charlotte was doing with a simple look and touch of her hand. Was this what true love felt like? He smiled gratefully at her before turning back toward his mother, whose eyes were pinned on them with an almost suspicious glint.

Annette cleared her throat. "When's the wedding?"

He wished he'd had more time to discuss the details with Charlotte, and Ivy for that matter. He hoped Ivy would stay still and not give them away with her own surprise and likely delight. They hadn't planned for pointed questions. He wanted to laugh. He hadn't planned at all. "Poor planning always leads to poor results" had been his professional mantra. When his mother changed her schedule, his plans went out the window.

Cricket sauntered over with pen and pad in hand. "What can I get ya?" She pointed her pen at Ivy. "I got you, little munchkin. Grilled cheese and tater tots, right?"

"Yes, please, and a chocolate milk?"

Annette gasped. "Nothing about that meal is healthy. Where are the vegetables?"

Ivy looked like she was ready to cry. Bastien knew from experience his mother's otherwise well-intentioned words embarrassed and criticized in a way only she could deliver them.

Bastien stepped in. "It's okay, Ivy. We're all here to enjoy ourselves, and that includes some fun food choices now and then. Right, Cricket?"

"It's got grain and dairy. I'm not feeding her a cup of sugar. Or a cup of warm cow shit," she said under her breath.

Annette cast a disapproving glance at Bastien. "Is there nowhere better to eat than this greasy spoon?" She snatched one of the paper napkins from the dispenser and placed it delicately over her lap. "One with real napkins?"

"Well, you're just honey on a hushpuppy, aren't you? I can see you're a woman with refined tastes. I've got a coffee you're gonna love." She jotted something down on her pad. "Poached salmon with a miso glaze served with fingerling potatoes and asparagus."

His mother smiled. "Oh. Seriously?"

Cricket laughed and shook her head, "Nope, it's fish and chips. You eat with your fingers. Those paper napkins will come in handy."

Bastien knew his mother was getting close to seeing the bottom of Cricket's shoe, rumored to have a middle finger drawn on the sole. "That sounds great to me." He turned to Charlotte. "What about you, honey?"

"I'll have the same."

Annette made a face. "All that grease is bad for the figure and the skin. You should be careful," she mused, looking at Charlotte. Bastien was happy Charlotte had not taken the bait. Annette perused the menu for several seconds. "I'll have a salad with chicken."

Cricket wrote their order on her pad and left.

"Now, where were we?" Annette glanced at each of them before settling her attention on Charlotte. "Oh, yes. The wedding. When is it?"

He turned his attention to Ivy, who seemed to not have paid much notice to the conversation while she folded paper napkins into some origami creation only a five-year-old could figure out.

When he looked at poor Charlotte, she resembled a deer caught in headlights for a moment, and then everything changed. She sat up and said, "We aren't spring chickens as you've noticed, so we planned to marry soon, but then my shop flooded, and everything has been delayed."

Bastien felt a knot in his stomach as he watched the emotion wash over Charlotte's face. He knew she was trying to put a brave face on things, but he could tell deep down she was sad and worried. He wanted to tell her everything would be okay, and he would do his best to make it so —for her.

He couldn't wait until they had a minute alone to find out why she'd stepped in. Not that he wasn't happy. In a perfect world where love actually mattered, he'd marry Charlotte in an instant, but this was fragile fiction where everything was complicated and uncertain and being made up as they went along. He didn't build his life or his business on improvisation, and he had now firmly departed from his comfort zone.

Cricket swung by and dropped off their drinks. Iced tea for him and Charlotte, chocolate milk for Ivy, and cat poop coffee for his mother. He only wished Cricket had a cup of warm cow shit to give her instead. Bastien knowingly waited with bated breath for her to take a drink, and when she did, he took great pleasure she had no idea what she was drinking.

Annette cleared her throat, bringing them both out of

their thoughts. "Oh." She picked up the cup and took another sip. "Kopi Lewak. I love this stuff. Finding it here is quite a surprise. It's rare and expensive."

Leave it to his mother to know just about everything, including about civet coffee. He placed his hand on Charlotte's. "Even better are things and people who are rare and priceless."

She smiled almost sincerely. "Let's get back to the wedding. How far along were your plans?"

"It was a work in progress. I had my dream wedding dress, but it was ruined by rusty pipe water from a leak next door to my shop." Charlotte closed her eyes as if she was envisioning it. "Ivory silk, with a train and hand-sewn beads that glittered in the light. The bodice was trimmed in lace so soft it felt like a lover's caress."

"Why was your wedding dress at your shop?" Annette asked. "What kind of business do you have?"

"Mom," Bastien replied. "Charlotte is the town's wedding planner."

"How convenient," she said with an air of suspicion.

"Plus, she's pretty and nice," Ivy added dreamily as she looked up at Charlotte as if she were the most amazing person in the world.

"That she is. Beautiful inside and out," Bastien said.

"Ivy, honey. Why don't you wash your hands before you eat," Charlotte said.

Somehow, Charlotte always had his back. She had Ivy's, too, by protecting her from hearing a conversation she was too young to understand.

Ivy climbed under the table and stopped beside him. "Can I have money for the jukebox?" He gave her a handful of quarters and watched her walk to the corner.

He hadn't considered how this might affect Ivy, but Charlotte had an impeccable sense of what he needed and when he needed it. Right now, he needed a frank conversation with his mom that wouldn't be heard by a five-year-old. He was confident that Tiffany wouldn't have had the maturity to see the situation for what it was—potentially upsetting and confusing to Ivy. Tiffany reminded him of the eager-to-please interns at his company. He was thankful that Charlotte had yanked him away from what would have been an unpleasant and unsatisfying connection, however short it may have been.

"When do you plan to get married?" Annette asked, jolting him from his thoughts.

"I'd marry Charlotte tomorrow if that were possible," he said.

"How about this weekend?" his mother suggested with a smile. "Just a small ceremony to make it official, and if you two want to have a bigger event later on, you can do a renewal of your vows."

Bastien was not expecting that. "What part of Charlotte being a wedding planner did you forget? She doesn't want a rushed wedding. If she wanted something fast, we could have gone to Vegas."

He glanced at Ivy dancing to "Everlasting Love" in front of the jukebox and cleared his throat. How poetic, he thought. He knew some of the lyrics. Something about opening your eyes and realizing that you're standing with your everlasting love. Chloe loved that song and played it for Ivy often. It seemed that Chloe wasn't the only one sending him a message. "If we marry this weekend, will you stop pushing for custody of Ivy?"

Annette sat back and smiled like a cat who'd devoured a

canary. "Are you saying you're only getting married to get custody?" she asked.

"I have custody. I don't need to get custody. Chloe already gave me that. You're trying to take it away. I don't need to marry to get something I already have."

"If you want me to give up the custody fight, I need to know this is more than just a business arrangement. How would it be for Ivy to have someone come into her life just to abandon her once they got what they wanted?"

Bastien and Charlotte exchanged a look. Had they gone through all the machinations for nothing? He knew his mother was sly. She'd even hired a private investigator.

"No one is going anywhere," Bastien said quickly. "Charlotte and I are perfect for each other." His face flushed with heat as he spoke the words aloud, knowing they were true. "What did your private investigator say?"

"He said you paid his monthly salary and sent me this picture." Without even a smidgeon of shame, she pulled out her phone and showed them the picture of them kissing on the beach. "When I showed up, I saw you with that other woman. I thought you were faking it." She stared at Charlotte. "Now, I'm not sure."

Charlotte reached for his hand and looked into Bastien's eyes. "I can assure you, I'm hopelessly in love with your son. While our relationship grew quickly, my love for him has been a slow burn since we met. He is kind, loving, intelligent, honorable, and steadfast."

His chest tightened as he heard her words. He knew she was probably reciting them for the money, but somehow, they made him feel so alive, and seen for the first time. Charlotte saw in him all things he strived so hard to be, but thought he often failed. He tried to push down his growing emotions, but he couldn't deny how incredible he felt with Charlotte at his side, describing all the things she'd gleaned in a few encounters to his mother, who had somehow missed them for a lifetime.

"How many times have you been married? You look a little mature to be holding off for a white wedding and bridesmaids," Annette quipped.

"Mother, how dare you!"

"It's OK, Bastien. It's a fair question if we are trying to get to know one another. I've never been married. I didn't see the point in settling when I knew my one true love would find me if I stayed true to myself and lived my life with kindness. What's the point of marriage if not to celebrate life in love together with all its trials? Bastien is the tiller in my roughest seas and the sunshine lighting my face in every waking moment."

Charlotte's words landed on Bastien's heart with a boom whether or not he wanted them to. He guessed for someone faking it, she deserved an Academy Award or maybe she was speaking her own heart. Maybe that was why everyone was telling him to open up his eyes.

"Well, that is quite a visual. Maybe on the seventh day, he'll rest. So, you were just waiting around for a single billionaire to show up?"

"Mother! Stop being insulting. You are talking to the woman I love!" With the conviction and clarity of a Southern Baptist preacher on a Sunday morning, he shouted his feelings before even knowing them himself. The words burst out of his heart and onto his tongue without the filter of thoughts to contain them. He turned quickly to see how they had landed with Charlotte. Her beaming smile told him everything he needed to know. Perhaps she was no longer playing a role, and neither was he.

"So sorry. How did you meet then?" Annette said in a sheepish retreat he had never seen from his mother.

Charlotte covered his hand as if to say, I've got this. Bastien was relieved she was more than holding her own in the grilling from Annette. "I live next door. Sadly, I didn't get to know Chloe because I'd been busy setting up my shop, but I brought them dinner one night, and that's how we met." She blushed and lowered her head. "Every time Bastien came to visit, he'd spend time on the shore, which is where we built our relationship. I have a little ritual of numbering things I find on the beach, and I offer them back to the sea with a wish." She pulled something from the pocket of her dress, and when she opened her palm, he saw a white and pink shell with a faded black number. Before he could say anything, Charlotte smiled. "I found a wish, and by my calculations, it's been tumbling in that water for close to thirty years." She rubbed at the almost-gone number.

"If it wasn't a single billionaire, what did you wish for?" Annette asked, seemingly trying hard to make a joke about her poor insinuation earlier. Bastien thought it could be a step in the right direction but did not hold out any hope that his mother would just give up.

Charlotte couldn't refuse her question without seeming resentful and standoffish. "Happiness."

He kissed her cheek. "How lucky are we? It was granted, for both of us." Bastien hoped he wasn't overselling, but it was exactly how he felt.

"Sorry for the delay." Cricket placed dishes on the table. When she put his mother's salad in front of her, she looked as if it were crawling in cockroaches. "This is fried chicken!"

"Welcome to the South, ma'am. Would you like a map

and guide to Southern manners with your salad dressing?" Cricket said with a chuckle.

His mother pushed the salad away. "I need to be off, anyway; I'm planning a wedding," she responded.

Cricket stepped back, surprised. "Oh? Who's getting married?"

Charlotte raised her hand, an ear-to-ear smile stretched across her beautiful face. "That'd be us. Me."

CHAPTER TWENTY-THREE

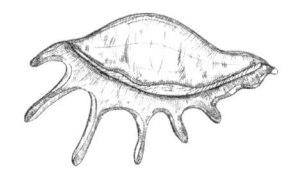

Charlotte heaved a sigh of relief when the tapping of Annette's stilettos went silent after the diner door closed behind her. She stared out the window and watched as Annette climbed into the back seat of the waiting cab and drove away. "Well, I thought that went a lot better than expected," she said, gazing at Bastien, awaiting his reaction.

"What just happened? I thought things were set with Tiffany. What don't I know?"

Charlotte let that question sit for a second. There was a lot he didn't know. She opened her mouth to speak, but Bastien spoke first.

"The words. Were they true?" Bastien's face lit up, but she couldn't tell if he was happy, anxious, or both. She reflected on his words too and felt what was becoming a familiar rush of warmth rise in her chest when she was near him.

"I believe you said I was the woman you love. We got engaged, and decided to get married next weekend, while eating fish and chips and watching Ivy dance," Charlotte offered, although she knew Bastien was looking for more.

"As for Tiffany ... I overheard your mother speaking to someone and insisting the woman with you in the diner wasn't the same one you were kissing on the beach." Ivy ran over and jumped into Charlotte's lap. "Where's Mee-maw?"

"Your grandmother had a long flight and felt tired. She said to say good night. Eat up. Uncle Bastien and I will take you home." Charlotte knew the conversation with Bastien about the exchange they'd just had with his mother was too important to conduct in hurried code in front of Ivy while she polished off her grilled cheese and tater tots. Besides, she would never talk about Ivy or her life as if Ivy were not in the room. She took Bastien's hand in hers and placed a gentle kiss on the fingers he'd wrapped effortlessly around hers, as if to say I know you are concerned, but this will have to wait for a private moment. She could see he understood and agreed.

"Come on, little ladybug. Let's finish up and get you home."

"Okay, Uncle Bast." Ivy popped a tater tot in her mouth. When she swallowed, she asked, "Can Charlotte sleep over?"

Charlotte blushed fifty shades of rose because there was nothing she would have wanted more, and she could see in Bastien's eyes and feel in his tightening grip of her hand he wanted that too. But Ivy came first for both of them, and Charlotte wasn't even sure Bastien meant the things he had said. "Not tonight, Ivy, honey, but we can all take a little walk on the beach if it's alright with Bastien." He squeezed her hand again in an enthusiastic yes, and after they finished their meal and left enough cash on the table to cover their tab, the trio headed for the door. "Good night," Cricket called after them with a wink. "Congratulations." Charlotte could see Cricket was barely containing her joy and what looked like a bit of self-satisfaction.

"Did you win a prize, Uncle Bast? How come Cricket said congratuwations?"

"It's congratu-la-tions, sweetie. And, yes, I won the best prize in life when I got to have dinner with Charlotte and you. And now I get to walk on the beach with the two most wonderful ladies I know." Charlotte admired his ability to answer Ivy honestly and avoid having to say too much.

"You're funny." Charlotte giggled at Ivy's assessment of her uncle and was grateful to be off the hook of fully explaining her actions and owning up to the things each had said, for the moment at least.

They left each other on the sidewalk and promised to meet at the water's edge.

As she drove, she reflected on what she knew: she loved him and was falling deeper and deeper each day. Thoughts that he might love her, and they could marry for real, dangled next to the knowledge that Bastien would do anything for Ivy and could have been putting on a show consistent with their plan—their agreement. She had bared her soul under the cover of Annette's interrogation. She could use that to dial things back if her declarations had been too much and Bastien didn't feel the same.

THE SKY WAS CLEAR, and the waves rolled softly onto the shore as she arrived at the beach. Ivy bounded toward the water's edge and immediately began sifting through the wet sand for treasures. "Look, Charlotte! I found a sand dollar. A whole one."

Bastien was close behind and ran to her side to verify

the find and move her away from the waves that seemed to get rougher all of a sudden. Charlotte watched in delight as he lifted her to the height of his waist and twirled her around and away from the sea until they were both safe and dry but dizzy. They fell to the sand laughing while Ivy clutched the sand dollar, and Charlotte ran over to join them.

She had underestimated the depth of the sand and stepped on her dress's hem, causing her to stumble and fall onto the soft sand too. She would have been embarrassed, but Bastien and Ivy laughing so hard filled her heart with so much happiness that she laid back and laughed as well. Especially at Ivy, who was now pretending to be a mermaid by holding her legs together and moving them like a tailfin while her hands elegantly weaved through the air. Her expression was focused, eyes glimmering, as if she was lost in an undersea world of her own.

The sun was setting and the cool air wafting above them signaled it was time to go in. "Alright, mermaids, it's time to get ready for bed," he said.

Charlotte's gaze caught Bastien's as he sprang upward and extended his hand to help her up from the sand. "I love being here like this. I love you." The words poured out of Charlotte's mouth with the same ease and joy as the laughter that preceded them.

Bastien didn't respond immediately. Instead, Charlotte noticed he was checking to see what Ivy had heard. Charlotte wanted to sink into the sand and be washed out to sea like one of her wishes. How could she have just let that slip out in front of Ivy? What was she thinking? What was she expecting? What happened to playing it cool, dialing it back, and letting everything sit for a time? She was such an idiot. She had forgotten that Bastien had every reason to wonder if the things she said were real. After all, she had accepted a payment to help solve his problem and then made a last-minute switch. He would protect Ivy at all costs, especially from someone who could leave her again.

"Good night, Charlotte," Ivy called, waving goodbye as Bastien walked with her toward the house and away from Charlotte. Bastien turned. "Aren't you coming? Ivy would love you to read and tuck her in. After, we can have a glass of wine."

Charlotte's heart pounded. What would happen once she got a glass or two of wine in her? Could she tell him about the conversation with Emmaline and have him believe, by coincidence, she had to oust Tiffany to protect his ruse?

She had already said too much or too much of the wrong thing. It always seemed strange to her that those three words could be an awakening salvation or the relationship equivalent of a nuclear bomb destroying everything in its wake and creating fallout that couldn't be overcome. She had heard them often enough but had never said them in the same way they had escaped her lips on the beach. At that moment, she meant I love you for who you are. I want you. I need you. Your happiness means as much, if not more, to me than my own. And I will cherish and protect you and our love forever. Charlotte realized she was much better at having these conversations with herself or Emmaline than with Bastien, but that was going to end tonight. She had to lay it all on the line. There was no longer any question about whether they would marry. Her bursting onto the scene at the diner and declaring her undying love for Bastien over fish and chips had left them with no "out." It wasn't as if he could say he'd changed his mind and loved Tiffany instead. Still, she had to know under what conditions they were getting married. Was it for love or money? That thought made her laugh. Of course, it wasn't for money in the way people usually thought, but in this case, people might get that impression. His mother wasn't shy about mentioning his billionaire status.

Once inside, Ivy got into her unicorn pajamas and brushed her teeth. She insisted on reading to Charlotte and not the other way around. Good thing, too, because Charlotte's mind continued racing, and she felt terrible about not being fully present for Ivy and the Adventures of Paddington Bear. When she finished the book, she placed it on the nightstand.

"Goodnight, Charlotte. I'm happy you love us. We love you too." She pulled the covers over her shoulder and turned on her side.

"I do love you. Sweet dreams, little bug." Charlotte kissed Ivy sweetly on the forehead and closed the door quietly as she left the room.

Bastien looked troubled sitting in the easy chair by the window. Two glasses of cabernet said he'd been waiting for her. "How's Ivy?"

"Fast asleep and so sweet. She read to me. I can't believe how well she reads. She's like a thirty-year-old trapped in a kid's body."

Bastien motioned for Charlotte to sit down, and she complied, although she was disappointed that they were sitting apart. She thought "I love you" should lead to snuggling and more, not exile to another piece of furniture, especially one that could easily hold them both while they held each other. He reached across to the sofa and handed her a glass of wine. She steeled herself with a fair gulp of the liquid courage and began, "Bastien, I have a confession to make."

He held up his hand to silence her. "Charlotte, I can't go on like this, just making it up as I go. It's not good for any of us."

Oh God. Charlotte braced herself for what would come next. They had just gotten engaged, sort of. Was he breaking up with her because she loved him? "I understand." She swallowed the lump in her throat and begged her eyes not to tear.

"I know I've put you in an impossible position, and I'm sorry," he continued. "I appreciate all you have done for Ivy and me." He paused.

"But?" Charlotte's head suddenly felt too heavy for her shoulders. Her eyes cast downward as tears welled, then fell to her cheeks no matter how hard she tried to defy gravity and hold them back. Was he giving up? On her? On Ivy? "Bastien, please let me explain." Charlotte composed herself and her thoughts. Like any well-raised Southern woman, she wasn't without grit. "I went to the diner intending to stop the marriage between you and Tiffany. And I would have done it even if I hadn't overheard your mother on the phone talking about how Tiffany wasn't the one you were kissing on the beach. I know it was wrong, and I will not accept your payment for an arrangement I broke on purpose. I'm sorry you'll have to pay Tiffany, but I will pay you back." Charlotte wasn't thinking about the pile of bills in her drawer, the insurance company refusing to compensate her losses on the store, or her house on the beach where generations of her family had played and sought refuge and that she would surely lose without Bastien's fee. None of it mattered when she had to tell Bastion how she felt or lose him forever.

"Bastien, I often fire before I aim. I jump into things without much thought or planning, but it's worked for me, and I can't imagine doing anything differently now when my heart says fire away. I love you—everything I know about you—and imagine as I get to know the rest, I'll love you even more. Not for today or tomorrow, but for all the moments of my life." She breathed out in relief at having let escape what had been building inside her since the moment she first laid eyes on this man stepping in to take care of his niece. "I don't care about a dream wedding, the dress I hoped I'd wear, or the chocolates. All I care about is you and Ivy. Please don't break up with me."

"Break up with you? I've always been a planner, but maybe that's the problem. I need more spontaneity in my life. I need to learn not to only trust my instincts, but also my heart. I'm not breaking up with you. I want to marry you, for love, life, and us, as well as Ivy. I love you too, and as crazy as it seems, it also seems right." He gently brushed a lingering tear from her soft cheek and knelt on one knee, extending his hands to reach hers. "Charlotte Sutton, I don't have ring, or a plan, but will you be my wife?"

There was only one answer, and she whispered, "Yes." She wanted to shout it so loud that it would be heard across the world, but that would wake Ivy, and while she was happy to share Bastien tonight, she wanted him to herself.

Bastien leaned forward and cupped her face tenderly. He traced his thumbs over her cheeks, with his eyes never leaving hers. His gaze was like a caress, a beautiful benediction that spoke volumes of love. His lips found hers, and he kissed her deeply, slowly, with a passion that seemed to be never-ending, yet was only the beginning.

Time slowed, and the room and its contents faded away as he led her to the bedroom and the bed. The moment had come to quench the hunger Bastien ignited when he'd kissed her for the first time. A craving that became only more and more intense the harder she tried to deny it. All that mattered was the two of them together. He laid her on the bed and kissed her again, this time more passionately and hungrily than before. The intensity of their desire for one another was palpable, like electricity arcing through the air. Bastien's hands roamed her body freely as he peeled the layers of her clothes away. He explored the soft curves of her waist, her breasts' soft swell, and her skin's smoothness. His touch was gentle and reverent.

"You're perfect," he said.

"You're crazy."

"Crazy for you."

She tugged at his clothes. "You're also wearing too much."

He chuckled. "I agree."

Charlotte felt a large lump between her shoulders and reached around, removing the unicorn backpack from underneath her. Suddenly she felt pulled back from her voyage as if she'd forgotten her passport. "What about Ivy?" Charlotte asked, barely able to find her breath.

Bastien smiled, never letting her go. "She sleeps like a cub in hibernation." Charlotte felt Bastien shift his weight before he stood. She was mesmerized by the sight of him. His body was a masterpiece, and she marveled at how perfectly sculpted it was. Even though she could feel her heart pounding, she felt safe and secure with him.

"Are you proposing we wait until Ivy is eighteen and at college? I don't think I can breathe another breath without knowing what it is to be inside you." He joined her, and soon they were lost in each other's embrace. Breathless, he pulled away from the kiss. "Am I rushing everything? I don't want to ruin it."

"The only way to ruin this is to stop." She shimmied her

body under his and gripped his hips. It had been a long time since she'd been intimate with anyone, but no one in her past had ever made her feel like there was a future. Bastien made her feel like hers was only possible with him.

"Make love to me," she whispered, barely loud enough for him to hear, but he heard, and he kissed her hungrily, as if in response to her plea before slowly entering her.

Charlotte was overcome with emotion as Bastien moved inside of her. His gentle yet passionate lovemaking made her feel cherished and adored. As he rocked against her, he unlocked parts of her she'd hidden away for far too long.

When the intensity peaked, Bastien leaned in and whispered, "I love you, Charlotte."

The sensation was overwhelming as they moved together in perfect harmony, each touch sparking something deep within their souls that bound them closer together. Every kiss and movement sent waves of pleasure washing over them like a gentle ocean tide until they reached the peak of bliss together before collapsing into each other's arms, totally spent, yet completely content.

At that moment, Charlotte realized that this man had become the center of her world, and she would do anything for him. She had found the peace and contentment she'd been searching for all along. It was right here in his arms.

CHAPTER TWENTY-FOUR

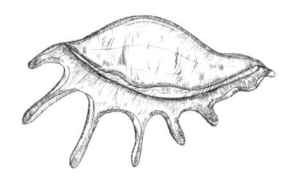

Bastien woke up with a smile on his face and Charlotte in his arms. After gently making love to her again, she dressed and left before Ivy woke.

As he readied Ivy's oatmeal, he grinned. He was getting married, and this time it was for real. Charlotte said yes.

"Hey, little bug. Guess what?"

Ivy was at the table eating oatmeal with chocolate chips, of course. "You love Charlotte?"

She was far too observant and would keep him on his toes for the rest of his life. "I do, and we are going to get married. Charlotte and I would love it if you'd be our flower girl."

"But I'm a ladybug."

The one thing he'd learned quickly was it was useless to argue with a five-year-old. "Very true and lady bugs like flowers, so what we're asking is if you'll be part of the wedding?"

"Can I wear a red dress?"

He didn't know what to say. Charlotte probably wouldn't care, but he knew that would send his mother into an early grave. "Let's talk to Charlotte about that later." He pulled her pigtails. Now that he'd learned to braid, she didn't want them anymore. "Time for school."

Ivy finished her oatmeal, brushed her teeth, and met him by the door with her knapsack. His plan today was all about putting things in order. First, he needed to pay Tiffany.

As they walked to the car, Charlotte rushed out. "I can take her. I've been summoned into town, anyway. Word has gotten around that I'm marrying this hot investment banker, and I'm in for a long inquisition." She turned to Ivy. "Honey, is it okay if I marry your uncle?"

"Will that make you my mommy?"

Bastien's heart sank into his gut. He wasn't sure how Ivy would feel about the marriage and hadn't even asked her if it was okay. He'd just assumed. He stared at Charlotte, wondering how she'd answer.

"No, honey, your mommy will always be your mommy. I'm not trying to take her place. I'll be Aunt Charlotte."

Ivy nodded, but a look of concern crossed her face. "Mommy told me that another mommy would eventually come and replace her, and it was okay. I'd be okay if you were my other mommy." She grabbed Bastien's hand. "Uncle Bast gets to be the daddy and then we're a family."

"You're right, we are a family." He opened the door and helped Ivy into the back seat. "I'll take her. I've got some stuff to get in order."

Charlotte nodded. "I bet. You haven't had time to process anything since Chloe's death. You probably have lots of probate stuff to deal with, too."

He hadn't thought about all the legal stuff.
He was just trying to take care of Ivy, but he figured it was

time to crack open Chloe's will. "I also need to pay Tiffany and buy an engagement ring for my bride-to-be."

She leaned in closer to him. "I don't need a ring. All I need is you." She leaned back and frowned. "I'm so sorry about Tiffany. I messed up this whole thing. Guess I'll need to leave matchmaking off my resume."

"I don't know. It worked out pretty well, I'd say." He kissed her. "Go hang with your friends. I'll be here when you get back." She turned to walk away, and he called out. "I love you."

When she smiled, his entire being felt complete. He'd accomplished a lot in his life, but nothing felt as gratifying as knowing the woman in front of him loved him back.

He made his way to Ivy's school and then drove to Sweet on You. He entered the shop and looked around for Marcus before he made his way to the counter.

"Be right with you," Tiffany said from the back. She appeared with a tray of chocolates that she slid into the glass display. "Oh, hey."

Bastien pulled the check he'd written early that morning from his pocket and set it on the glass top. "I wanted to bring this to you."

She looked at the total, and her eyes grew large. "It's more than we agreed to and besides, I didn't finish my part of the deal."

He chuckled. "No, you were sidelined."

She smiled. "Seems to me like my replacement is a better choice." Tiffany picked up the check. "Do you love her?"

He closed his eyes and relived that last kiss. It was quick but held the promise of forever. "I do."

She set the check back on the display case. "I can't take this. It's not right."

"It's right for you." He looked around once more to make sure Marcus wasn't within earshot. "You deserve better. Use this to help you get what you want, need, and deserve. If not for you, then for Ava." He turned around and walked toward the door.

"Hey, Bastien?"

He swung around to face her. "Yes?"

"You would have made a great fake husband."

He smiled. "I'll make a better real one for Charlotte."

He left the candy store, not feeling poorer for the sizable check he wrote but richer for all that he'd gained.

"Bastien?" He turned to find his mother walking toward him. In her hands was a Cricket's Diner to-go cup.

"Mother. What are you doing here?"

She held up the cup. "It's the only place to get a decent cup of coffee. And worth the thirty-dollar charge."

He hadn't eaten breakfast and thought a solid meal was wise before he dove into the will. "I was going to get something to eat. Would you care to join me?"

His mother waved her hand in the air. "Who has time to eat when there's a wedding to plan?"

He sighed. "Mother, Charlotte is a wedding planner. Like every woman, she probably had big dreams for her big day. Why the rush?"

"Because life is uncertain. Do you think your sister thought she was going to die?"

"She knew she had limited time, which is why she was so adamant about getting Ivy settled."

Her mother looked up at him and raised her chin. "She didn't even say goodbye."

"Neither did you when you walked out on Ivy at the diner. There isn't a team of people here to back you up when you leave without explanation."

"Were you going to get married without inviting me or your father?"

He wanted to laugh, but it was too sad a situation. "My father couldn't be bothered to come to Chloe's funeral." He sent flowers and his condolences as if she were an acquaintance, and he supposed she was as he had little to nothing to do with them except donate to their DNA. Part of him wished maybe they were the pool boy's children, but he knew better.

"I'm going through her will if you'd like to join me." He hadn't meant to invite her, but he imagined she needed to see it too. Maybe reading Chloe's wishes would make her drop her desire for custody.

"No, thank you." She reached inside her purse. "You were on my list to visit today." She made a face and shook her head. "If you intend to marry Charlotte, put a ring on her finger. I noticed she wasn't wearing one. What kind of man proposes without a ring? I thought at least some of your upbringing would have stuck." She opened a vintage filigree-trimmed leather box, revealing his grandmother's diamond wedding set and the Boucheron stamp inside. "It's a priceless family heirloom, so don't give it to her if your heart isn't in it." She snapped the box closed and handed it to him. "I hope you're doing this for love and not to win. That's something your father would do. You're his namesake but have always tried to prove you were nothing like him. Don't be like him now."

He'd been named Sebastien at birth, but he legally changed his name to Bastien. His whole life he'd been trying to prove himself different and he'd almost repeated his father's actions and married for obligation. The fact didn't change that he was marrying Charlotte, but now he knew it wasn't only for Ivy's sake. It was for his as well.

"Thank you. Charlotte will be touched. She is sentimental and this will mean a lot to her. It would mean more if she knew you were giving it with your blessing and love too."

His mother smiled sadly. "Ah, what do I know about love?" She walked away, leaving him to wonder what had gone wrong. Had she never been loved? She hadn't been shown any love by her husband or her children. After all, they'd only been allowed home visits now and then.

He tucked the ring box inside his pocket. Rather than go to Cricket's, he headed straight home to read the will.

EATING one of Ivy's cinnamon Pop Tarts, he sat in the living room, staring at the big envelope that had his name written in Chloe's distinctive handwriting. Whereas his was hardly legible, she made her letters full of flourishes that made them stand out and look like art. That was how Chloe was. She was a standout.

Time ticked by as he looked at the envelope and he realized this was a tear the Band-Aid off quickly moment, so he opened it and pulled out the stack of papers and other closed envelopes inside. On top was a hand-written letter.

Dear Bastien,

I could spend pages telling you how angry I am that cancer won, but we both know that living in the past is a waste of time. This is all about the future. Yours. Ivy's. Mom's.

He was surprised to find his mother mentioned and continued reading.

> How do you like the beach house? I hope you'll stay. Ivy loves it here. We started collecting seashells. I told her that our bodies were like shells and eventually we outgrew them and left them behind. She understands that I'm gone, and that life will go on. I've assured her that while I've left my shell behind, my spirit will live in her forever, and that is why I asked you to take care of her. It's not that Mom doesn't mean well, it's that she doesn't know any better. You know better. You know what it's like to love because I've felt the love you've given me and Ivy, and it's the gold standard.
>
> If you can, I have a bunch of requests that I'd love you to fulfill. You're a man who's always driven to succeed, so I'm certain you won't give anything less than your best effort.
>
> Make sure Ivy knows I love her.
>
> Give mom a chance. You'll find in the will that I've given her visitation rights. Our mother on a full-time basis is more than anyone can handle. Maybe she knew that early on, and that's why she sent us away. Despite her

faults, she has a lot to offer Ivy. Mom, if nothing else, is the epitome of a well-bred lady, and that's something you can't help Ivy become.

If you decide to leave Willow Bay, keep the house for Ivy, so she'll always have a place to call her own. In the short time we were here, we built a lot of memories. I hope she'll build many more.

My dear brother, have you ever thought of falling in love? It might be my only regret. While I had lots of love in my life from you and Ivy and friends, I wish that I'd opened myself to the idea of loving someone else. Someone who could hold me at night and wake with me in the morning. They say life is so much richer when shared. Find someone to share your life with. Get yourself a partner and choose carefully, for she will become Ivy's mother, and you know me; I would only want what is best for my little girl.

Last, live life to the fullest. We never know when it will be cut short. When I was lying in that bed, I never thought one moment of money or things. All I thought about was if I'd loved those around me enough.

I love you.

Chloe

He sat there for a moment while a tear slid down his cheek. "You did, sis. You loved us enough." He glanced through the papers, which included a custody agreement and the deed to the house, which she'd put in trust for Ivy. His sister had thought of everything from her college fund to her birthdays, for which she'd written a letter to celebrate each year until Ivy turned eighteen. She'd even thought of Ivy's future wedding day, if she married, by writing her a letter for that life moment, too.

As he tucked them back into the larger envelope, he thought about his sister's requests. The hardest would be his mother, but he was willing to offer an olive branch if she would take it.

He pulled the ring box from his pocket and opened it, surveying not just the diamonds but the unexpected sentiment from his mother that had accompanied them. The setting was simple and elegant like Charlotte, and he hoped she would like it. If not, he'd buy her any ring she wanted. He imagined she'd have at least one joke about her ring being able to fill in as the beacon if the lighthouse power went out. It was a large stone, but its simplicity made it refined, not garish. On reflection, he knew she would love it. He tucked it into his pocket and walked outside to find a shell to throw into the sea. Today he'd cast the biggest wish of all. He'd wish for a lifetime of happiness for everyone, including his mother.

As he scoured the shore for the perfect shell, he heard tires on gravel and turned expecting Charlotte, but it wasn't her getting out of the car; it was a group of women and they looked like they meant business. But what business? Couldn't be a religious group. They sent young men in suits, and arrived on bikes, not luxury sedans. Green Peace proffered naturalist-looking millennials in Priuses. Maybe it was the local auxiliary looking for donations for the bake sale? The leader of the posse approached him, and he recognized it was Marybeth, Charlotte's friend, who had visited him and Ivy from the church.

"Bastien?" Marybeth called out as she and the other two marched toward him. "You don't get to marry Charlotte without asking her friends first."

His eyes grew wide. He'd heard of getting permission from the father, but the girlfriends? "I'm sorry for overstepping my boundaries. I thought love was all I'd need."

That seemed the right thing to say because when they got to him, they didn't brandish weapons, only smiles and congratulations. "Can we talk?" Marybeth asked.

He led them into his house. If Charlotte's friends were going to talk, he was going to listen. As soon as they were inside, the woman named Tilly went to work making a pot of coffee while the other women peppered him with questions about his intentions, his history, how he had proposed, what plans he'd made already. As they sipped coffee, Marybeth cleared her throat. "Since we were kids, Charlotte had a dream of being married on the beach. How would you feel about that?"

"I'd marry Charlotte anywhere."

"Wonderful. We don't have much time to prepare her perfect wedding but we're going to try. Between us, we can handle caterers, the preacher, chairs, flowers, and the rest. But there's one thing we can't possibly deliver."

"What's that?"

"Charlotte's dress. It would take an act of God, and even my connection isn't good enough," Marybeth said with a chuckle. "The dress Charlotte had made for her 'someday' was on display in Because You Said Yes when it was flooded. We wouldn't know where to begin. Everything from the lace to the interlining was custom. Only someone with connections to a premiere couture house would be able to come close on short notice. That dress was the embodiment of Charlotte's dream wedding, assuming she found her dream man. That's you. I can guarantee you this will be the only wedding Charlotte will ever have. Of course, she would marry you in anything, but we all know how much that beautiful gown meant to her. What do you think? Would you help us?"

He thought about his sister's letter and her request to give his mom a chance. Annette was always boasting about her ability to get anything done, solve any problem, find the tiniest needle in the largest haystack, and for damn sure she knew people in haute couture. He'd put her to the test. "I know the perfect person for the job. Leave me your numbers."

"Then leave the rest to us. And don't say a word. It's a long shot." They didn't know his mother. Nothing was a long shot to Annette Richmond, Bastien thought with a hint of pride that surprised him. When they left, he phoned his mother and before she could say anything, he said, "Mom, I could use your help."

There was a moment of silence before she said, "You what? You need my help?" Her voice sang. It felt to him as if she'd been waiting to be wanted or needed her whole life. "Yes, of course. Anything, Bastien. Shall I come now?"

CHAPTER TWENTY-FIVE

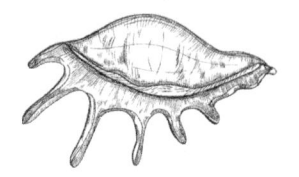

Charlotte took a long look at herself in the mirror and smiled. This wasn't her dream wedding, but she didn't care. She was getting her dream man. While the dress was pretty, its modern edginess was better suited to Emmaline. It seemed a lifetime ago that her friend walked ... no, ran ... barefoot down the aisle in the same dress to Miles, but it was just a few short months ago.

For a wedding in a flash, Annette and her friends had pulled off a miracle. She hadn't expected anything more than to exchange vows on the beach with Bastien. But when she arrived at The Kessler, the extravagance of creativity, energy, and heart that everyone had expended was obvious and touched her deeply. Besides the dress, she didn't think she could have done better herself, even with more time.

Tilly was catering the event, and Marybeth had filled the venue with gorgeous flowers. Marybeth wasn't one to let anything go to waste. Charlotte wondered if they might be leftovers from a funeral and thought that it would be fine if they were. In many ways, funerals were no different from weddings for the intensity of love they celebrated. And if it were not for a funeral, she would have never met the love of her life.

A sharp knock echoed from the door, a first-floor suite of The Kessler. "Come in," Charlotte called. No one knew she was there except her friends, who'd given her a few minutes to herself.

When Annette opened the door, she was caught off guard. "Annette," Charlotte uttered in surprise.

Annette was far from the mother-in-law she had imagined, but she had to admit she was warming a tiny bit to her quick wit. She was grateful not just for Bastien being on Earth, but also for being the catalyst for his search for a wife. Her dreams of a mother-in-law who would welcome her as a daughter of her own would have to come true in another lifetime. Annette and Charlotte shopping, cooking, and decorating together was as unlikely as a pig flying in Louboutins. Her smile at the image that had popped up quickly turned to sadness as her parents' absence emptied her full heart for a moment. She breathed it in and then let it go. This was a day for joy. Still, she wished her parents had lived to share her special day. Without her father to give her away, she'd be walking down the aisle alone.

Annette examined Charlotte from head to toe, her smile turning to a look of disappointment. "Look at you." She shook her head. "It's all wrong."

Charlotte shifted her weight from one foot to the other, her heart thudding against her ribcage. *Here we go*, she thought. Just when she thought it might be safe to go in the water, here came Jaws. She glanced down at the improvised dress she hadn't chosen—it was a more "hip" wedding dress and nothing like the elegant ivory gown she had imagined herself wearing. She continued to convince herself that it would do. Bastien would marry her in a potato sack. That much she knew. Enough, she told herself. She wasn't a little girl. She could move past her fantasy because the reality of her future was so much more than she had ever dreamed.

"I don't know. It's not the dress I dreamed of, but it will do." With a deep breath, she looked in the mirror and resigned herself to the fact that this was the dress she would wear.

Annette's eyes narrowed as she studied Charlotte. She moved around her, pulling and tugging at the gown, her forehead creased with a frown. "No, it won't work," she said firmly. "If there's one thing I know for certain, you don't lie to yourself or make compromises on your wedding day. You wouldn't go to a friend's wedding in a dress you didn't like. How will you feel when you see the pictures of you in something that's not you? It will be like a bad haircut you have to see for the rest of your days. Take it off."

It wasn't Annette's fault that Charlotte's dream wedding gown had been ruined, but did she have to criticize her so harshly on her wedding day? Especially while she was missing her mother and father so profoundly. Her gaze pierced through Annette, her fury clear and present. "I can't. It's all I have for today."

Annette stepped closer, her fingers tugging on the zipper. "You'd be happier in a gunny sack and ten times as attractive. This thing is shaped like a satin condom, for heaven's sake. Twinkies have more 'line.'" The surrounding air suddenly went arctic, a spark of rage igniting in Charlotte's eyes.

Charlotte's palms started sweating as she faced off with Bastien's mother. She could feel the heat rising, her temper flaring as the woman stood there looking down her nose at her. "I know you don't like me, but..." Charlotte balled her hands into fists, her voice rising, "I was starting to appreciate your wit and elegance, and we both love your son. So, let's get along for his sake." Her words seethed with venom, and she could see the shock in Bastien's mother's eyes before she continued. "I'm glad you're here because I'd like to start my marriage to Bastien off right and lying to his mother isn't the way to go." Charlotte took a deep breath, steeling herself for the next words that would change their lives forever. "You were right. We were faking the marriage."

Annette laughed. "Oh, honey, you're mistaken if you think you faked anything."

Charlotte watched her intently, utterly perplexed, trying to decipher the meaning behind her words. Most likely, they hadn't pulled the wool over her eyes. "I'm sorry we tried to fool you. We only wanted to ensure that Chloe got what she wanted for Ivy. She wanted Bastien to raise her, and you pointed out that he wasn't married, so we thought..."

"The only one you were fooling was yourself. One look at my son, and I knew. I may not have been the perfect mother, but despite what they thought, I loved my kids and always knew what was happening with them."

"You knew he was lying."

Annette shook her head. "No, I thought he might be, which was why I hired the private detective, but looking at him looking at you, I knew he was in love. I saw it in the photo from the beach. You don't think I know Bastien's eyes? Of course, I do."

"Oh." She had read the situation all wrong. Annette wasn't coming in at the last minute to knock Charlotte off the altar and run away with Ivy.

Annette stood behind Charlotte, carefully unzipping the back of the dress as a mother would do for her daughter's first prom. As the garment dropped to the floor, Charlotte stood in only her white lace bra, underwear, and heels. Annette then walked to the door and quickly returned with a garment bag.

Annette beamed as she said, "Your wedding day is one of the most important days of your life. You deserve it to be perfect in every way, and you should have the perfect dress." She lifted the garment bag with a whoosh, hung it at the top of the door, and unzipped it. The teeth of the zipper clicked, slowing one by one until the opening revealed what looked exactly like Charlotte's own stunning wedding gown.

Charlotte gasped. She strode toward it, letting her fingertips brush over the beaded lace bodice. "How did you get my dress?" she asked.

Annette chuckled. "Annette Richmond never takes no for an answer," she said as she removed the ivory gown from its hanger and helped Charlotte step into it. "You should never settle. Not when it comes to men, and not when it comes to dresses." She zipped up the back and beamed at her. "It's a perfect fit, just like you for my son and granddaughter. You look simply stunning."

Charlotte tried to hold back the tears, but one still trailed down her face. There was one more tough subject to discuss. "If I'm the best choice for Ivy, does that mean you won't be challenging Bastien for custody?"

Annette exhaled deeply and stepped away. "I owe everyone an apology, but I'm not good at that, and I'm certainly not going to try now. Suffice it to say, the pain of losing my daughter was unbearable. I was lashing out and had convinced myself Ivy was better with me. In a few short weeks, you seem to have accomplished what no woman has come near in almost three decades—the taming of Bastien Richmond. Anyway, Bastien was correct; I'm too old to be a parent to a five-year-old. After spending only a few hours with Ivy, I felt like I had completed a marathon. Trying to keep up with that child is like trying to catch the wind. It's simply not possible," she said, eyeing Charlotte's ring. "That was my mother's, and I hope it brings you luck and joy. She was a formidable woman, beautiful and creative like you."

Charlotte let her finger float lightly over the smooth surface of the enormous rock, thinking about when Bastien knelt by the shore and asked for her hand in marriage for the second time. She accepted, and they then took a shell and threw it into the ocean, wishing happiness for all. Even though the shell hadn't returned, Charlotte felt their wish had been granted.

"Thank you," she whispered.

Annette leaned in and kissed Charlotte's cheek. "No, darling. I'm the one who should thank you. You've brought me something I have been missing for a while now—hope and a family." She walked towards the door, but then stopped and turned. "I'll send your friends in." She pulled the door open, but before she stepped out of the room, she added one last thing: "Ivy is insisting she wear her red dress."

"I'm learning to pick my battles. Her fashion choice is a battle I'm likely to lose," Charlotte said. "At least she'll match the roses."

Annette left, and a few minutes later, her friends appeared.

"Oh, my God," Emmaline squealed. "That's the prettiest dress ever. How did she do that?"

Charlotte thought about Annette. "My mother-in-law is a force of nature."

Marybeth said, "It's best to stay in her good graces," as

she lifted the veil and placed it atop Charlotte's head. She added, "I'll be sending prayers your way."

Tilly grabbed the bouquet and handed it to her. "I'd appreciate it if you could keep these away from me when you're throwing them later," she said. "I want to steer clear of whatever wedding bug you all have." Tilly was the last firefly left without a partner. Charlotte had assumed they'd be old maids together, but life had brought her a prince; maybe there was someone out there for Tilly too.

Annette peered into the room. "It's time," she said.

Charlotte looked at her friends and made a final decision. "Annette, you are responsible for this day in many ways, and I'm so grateful for everything you've poured into our marriage. It would be a great honor if you would walk me down the aisle."

Annette smiled. "The honor is all mine, Charlotte. Thank you," she said, holding back tears.

"Oh my, where's little Ivy?" Charlotte said to her friends, who were also holding back tears. "I'm ready when you are. All we need is Ivy, and we're set to go."

Annette laughed. "That one's slippery as an oil slick. She was just here."

Soon after, Ivy stepped into the room wearing her red dress adorned with ladybugs stitched on the pockets. Her hair was braided, and in her hands, she held a basket meant to be filled with rose petals but instead was filled with a collection of tiny seashells.

"Where are the flower petals?" Marybeth asked. "I filled your basket up with red roses."

Ivy shook her head. "Mommy would want to be here, so I put shells."

Marybeth gave Charlotte a look. "Oh, I'm going to need

to pray for you. You will require Samson's strength and Abraham's serenity to raise that child."

Charlotte smiled and placed her hands on Ivy's shoulders before leaning down and kissing her rosy cheek. "I think shells are the best idea yet," she said with a glint in her eye. She reached for Ivy's hand and opened the door, ushering her into the hallway. "Uncle Bast is waiting. You go ahead of us and sprinkle your shells. Mee-maw and I are going to walk together and follow you." A thrill ran through Charlotte as she imagined the possibilities of the adventure they were about to embark on.

Charlotte made her way through the lobby and outside to the aisle where Bastien and the preacher were waiting at the end. The area was filled with people from her hometown. Cricket was sitting in the first row dressed up but still in her famous red high tops. The sun was shining, and birds were chirping around them. To the right, there was a picturesque setting with covered tables and crystal glassware—prepared for the upcoming reception—but all Charlotte could think of was how she felt in her dream wedding dress, ready to marry her dream man.

Emmaline reached over and squeezed Charlotte's hand to give her strength. This was it—the moment she had waited for all her life. Taking a deep breath, Charlotte stepped down the aisle that would take her to the man she would marry. She couldn't quite make out the music in the background—the pounding of her heart drowned it out.

The music swelled, and the guests rose from their seats as Charlotte approached Bastien, with Annette on one side beaming proudly and Ivy by her side, spreading her seashells like tiny treasures. Annette took her seat in the front row, leaving Charlotte at Bastien's side. Ivy stayed at the altar, so she didn't miss a thing. He welcomed them with open arms that engulfed them and a smile that told Charlotte he thought he was the luckiest man on earth. Charlotte felt she could float away if Bastien hadn't been there to hold her. Yes, true love had found her; it was as magical as she always dreamed it would be.

Charlotte's voice wavered as she repeated her vows, and tears glittered in her eyes. All the emotions of a lifetime seemed to be concentrated at this moment; all her dreams of love and family unfolded before her eyes.

Finally, it was time for them to seal their union with a kiss. As their lips met and the guests rejoiced, Charlotte knew she would cherish this moment forever—the start of something beautiful that would last a lifetime! She had never felt so carefree. Life and love were hers for the taking. As his wedding gift to her, Bastien had paid for all the misfortunes weighing her down. He insisted she had kept up her end of the agreement, and it was only fitting they begin their shared life without worry. He did not want bills, mortgages, or insurance companies peering from the back of Charlotte's mind into the happiest day of their lives.

She looked into Bastien's eyes and asked, "How did I get so lucky?" She'd gotten him, Ivy, and the life she'd always hoped for.

He held her tight and smiled, gazing into her eyes. "Because you said yes."

OTHER BOOKS BY KELLY COLLINS

An Aspen Cove Romance Series

One Hundred Reasons

One Hundred Heartbeats

One Hundred Wishes

One Hundred Promises

One Hundred Excuses

One Hundred Christmas Kisses

One Hundred Lifetimes

One Hundred Ways

One Hundred Goodbyes

One Hundred Secrets

One Hundred Regrets

One Hundred Choices

One Hundred Decisions

One Hundred Glances

One Hundred Lessons

One Hundred Mistakes

One Hundred Nights

One Hundred Whispers

One Hundred Reflections

One Hundred Chances

One Hundred Dreams

One Hundred Desires

GET A FREE BOOK.

Go to www.authorkellycollins.com

ACKNOWLEDGMENTS

This book would never have existed if it weren't for my sister Terry. She aided me every step of the way and motivated me to keep writing. I owe this entire work to her.

ABOUT THE AUTHOR

International bestselling author of more than thirty novels, Kelly Collins writes with the intention of keeping love alive. Always a romantic, she blends real-life events with her vivid imagination to create characters and stories that lovers of contemporary romance, new adult, and romantic suspense will return to again and again.

For More Information
www.authorkellycollins.com
kelly@authorkellycollins.com

Printed in Great Britain
by Amazon